Scarlet Yearnings

STORIES
OF
LOVE AND DESIRE

Scarlet Ibis James

DKJ Enterprises LLC

Praise for Scarlet Yearnings

WINNER of the 2025 International Impact Book Award
Finalist for the 2025 American Legacy Book Awards

For Adult Readers Interested in Emotional Stories – "Through these captivating narratives, Scarlet Ibis James takes a deep dive into the intricate relationship dynamics between people, illustrating both the highs and lows of relationships in all their myriad forms." –Readers Favorite

This Book Is a Great Read – "Each story explores a different facet of what it means to love and be loved, conveying the layered intricacies of individual relationships." – Jamie Tukpah, Bookium

Love and Complexity – "The author doesn't shy away from the messy, complicated side of love. It's refreshing." – The Bourbon-Sipping Bibliophile, Goodreads Reviewer

Stories That Stay With You – "Courage is a quality I admire—and worry I don't have enough of. These stories made me reflect deeply on my own decisions." – Amanda Jones, Author

Dare to Love Again – "Scarlet Yearnings accomplishes something surprisingly rare in contemporary short fiction – it makes us feel the full impact of love's complexities without relying on melodrama or easy sentiment." – Maria Ashford, BookShelfie

To C. Elyse, a fellow traveler on this writer's path.

Contents

Foreword

Love has always been the language I wanted to learn, but it is the one I speak the least fluently.

I trace this back to a time when I was just a child—a child who was never claimed by a father, whose mother gave her away. There has always been a space within me, vast and yearning, that longs to be desired, to be claimed, to be drenched in love from head to toe.

I sought every book by the romantic fiction publishing houses of Harlequin and Mills & Boon. Later, I found myself addicted to Hallmark movies and K-dramas. I loved love.

Consuming those love stories has always been my way of filling that void and soothing the aching desire for what was never mine.

With this collection, I've poured that longing into twelve stories. Each one is a testament to the kind of love I have sought and continue to pursue. But within each tale, you will also find an unsatisfied yearning—a reflection, perhaps, of the longing that still resides in me. These stories are not just narratives; they are pieces of my soul, fragments of my deepest desires.

As you turn these pages, I hope you find something within these stories that resonates with your own heart. Perhaps in reading them, you'll claim a piece of the love I have always sought, and in doing so, you'll help me find the acceptance I've longed for. This collection is as much a gift to you as it is a journey of reclaiming my desires.

May these stories touch you, stir you, and perhaps even leave you with a lingering sense of longing - just as they have for me.

Scarlet Yearnings returns in this new edition, featuring a beautifully artistic cover and an expanded story that dives deeper into marital desire. Scarlet Ibis James explores love's many shades—from sweet hope to bittersweet longing—offering thought-provoking snapshots of the heart's complex terrain.

The First Time She Met Her Father

"What's your favorite color?" he asked in a booming voice, making Trisha's body tremble.

She giggled and looked up sideways at him through her dark curls before saying, "Red."

This was the first time she met the person Granny said was her 'daddy.'

She wondered what he would want to know about her next.

She hoped he would ask, "If you could have any superpower, what would it be?"

Ready for this question, she would have said, "To make you want me."

But he asked, "Did you go to school today?"

And, "Do you listen to your grandmother?"

Then, "Do you play nicely with your friends?"

She answered "Yes," to all his closed-ended questions.

He turned away then, but Trisha smiled and giggled shyly as he joked with and hugged his mother before inhaling all the food she had cooked for him.

He devoured the fried *Cascadura* fish, tearing through the crispy skin to the tender meat, then moved on to the macaroni pie, scooping it up with callaloo. Each bite was swift and focused, as if he were racing to clear his plate.

Trisha watched, hoping he'd notice the bright napkins and the single red *Hibiscus* flower she'd set on the table, but his eyes were glued to his mother, creasing at the edges with every laugh they shared.

Trisha watched and waited for him to feel the pull of her desire for him.

"Ma, you really outdid yourself," he said, wiping his mouth with the back of his hand.

His mother beamed. "I had to, didn't I? Only the best for you."

He chuckled, stood up, and hugged her tightly. "You spoil me."

Trisha's heart sank as he turned to leave, his eyes never once glancing at the little details she had fussed over, left unnoticed in the wake of his easy affection for his mother.

Then, she observed as he buckled up a little girl whom she had only just come to know as her baby sister. She stared as he opened and closed the door for his wife and followed his movements as he slid into the red car.

The First Time She Met Her Father

He looked out the window and asked, "Will you be a good girl for your grandmother?"

Her smile never faltered when she answered, "Yes."

That day, when she met her father, Trisha learned to smile even as her heart broke — it was also the day she came to hate the color red.

Scarlet Ibis James

Love Me, Daddy

I saw him from my perch on the tall stool in the Harlem coffee shop. Gazing through the immense, age-stained window, I overlooked the wide sidewalk of the busy intersection.

The tall, lanky man with dirty blond hair, wearing a jet-black long wool coat glided into view. My eyes snagged on him, pupils involuntarily widening to take in his imposing figure.

Are you the healing balm I need? I wondered.

The ache of my recent breakup was still fresh. Yet, with a primal urgency, my body and mind were already restless, searching for a new connection. It felt like a base instinct—a desperate need to fill the void left behind.

My best friend would say I had Daddy issues. Yeah, I'd say so too.

Daddy wasn't just my father. He was my biggest cheerleader. Whenever I doubted myself, whether it was nailing that piano audition or starting my own business, he'd ruffle my locs and say, "You've got this, princess. You always do."

Even now, five years after he passed away, when I face a tough decision, I can practically hear his ghost voice in my head. That gruff but gentle encouragement pushed me forward. I miss him.

In my mind's eye, I could see my father. He loved wearing black wool coats. He had about five of them, hanging in a neat row in his closet like silent sentinels. I never knew where he got them all or why he needed so many, but they seemed to hold a piece of him, a secret story woven into the thick black fabric. The scratch of the wool against my cheek as he hugged me goodbye is a feeling I can still recall.

He would smile that bright white smile framed by thick, black, cigarette-stained lips. Ingrown hair leathered his rough cheeks. He was dark-skinned from head to toe — his salt-and-pepper curls crowned by that unruly mane of hair.

Every inch of his frame spoke of a life spent working hard, selling door to door for that insurance company. It was a sacrifice made with love for a family he cherished more than any raise or promotion.

But this man passing by me now was nothing like my Daddy. He was what my father would avoid: professional, obviously affluent, overly WASPy, and unapologetically White.

Why are you looking at that White boy? My father's voice in my head made me blink and look away.

Still, I wondered why that man caught my attention. I had always preferred men who were Black.

Unbidden, the slideshow of my exes ticked through my mind.

Click. Kwame, my first love in college, balanced a worn leather satchel overflowing with textbooks. His brow furrowed in concentration, a faint melody humming beneath his breath, proof of his dual passions: astrophysics and jazz saxophone.

Click. Ezrah sat on the porch in the southern town where I interned, his weathered hands carving intricate designs into a piece of driftwood. Laugh lines crinkled around his eyes as he shared lie after lie of adventures he never had.

Click. Darius, the corner store owner, greeted everyone with a booming, "How you doin' today?" His worn baseball cap barely contained his salt-and-pepper curls, and his smile lit up the whole shop. I regretted hooking up with him days after my father passed. Now I had to avoid this convenience shop.

Click. Jason, a skinny teenager, dribbled the basketball with practiced ease. Don't judge me—he was a mature nineteen-year-old. I loved tasting the sweat beaded on his forehead as we tangled. His eyes gleamed with determination as he aimed to please me.

Click —

"That clock's ticking is loud, isn't it?" his voice floated into my right ear like sweetened cream thickened with gelatin and flavored with vanilla. I turned to see the same White man I was ogling sitting on the stool beside me.

Only now did I hear the tick-tock of the clock. Each tick had been another memory clicking by, but now, all other faces were forgotten. I saw only the man next to me.

"Um...."

"I've rendered you speechless?" he asked, smiling.

I stared at him, wide-eyed, unable to say or do anything.

"Oookay," he said before breaking our eye-lock and turning to look out the window as I had been doing moments before.

My eyes glided down his torso, taking in the entire length of his black wool coat before cascading back up his body and resting on his gorgeous face.

I stared, knowing this young Leonardo DiCaprio look-alike would be in a slideshow starting soon.

My cheeks tingled in anticipation of the soft wool scraping gently against my skin, a primal urge to absorb his scent and feel the comforting texture against my face.

Love in Cosmic Times

Tessa

I shielded my eyes against the twin suns' glare, watching as the shimmering arcs of the orbital taxis traced their familiar paths across the azure sky — a mundane sight in this age, yet a reminder of how far humanity had journeyed among the stars.

Tessa, is your love destined to drift aimlessly within this unbridgeable gap, unable to touch him in real life?

This question haunted me as I stood on the threshold of my quiet life, contemplating the enigmatic relationship I shared with Wright, who lived far beyond Earth's edges.

Our connection had bloomed in my dreams of reaching beyond the ordinary. It all began when I decided to venture into the old world of digital dating, seeking a connection that could transcend the limits of my everyday existence.

One fateful day, while swiping through profiles that seemed otherworldly, I stumbled upon Wright's profile. It felt like destiny had intervened. He was an adventurous soul, and our match felt serendipitous, filling me with excitement.

We began exchanging messages, and every word felt like a revelation. We shared stories of our dreams and our yearning for a love that could bridge the divide between us. Wright's messages were filled with curiosity and mystery, drawing me in with each response.

Months passed by in a whirlwind of digital conversations. We laughed, confided in each other, and shared our deepest desires and fears. It was as if our souls had found a way to connect through the screen, and I couldn't help but feel that we were meant to be.

We decided to take the next step in our relationship. With the help of a video app, we met face-to-face for the first time. My heart raced with anticipation as the screen seemed to vanish, leaving only Wright's image before me. Our eyes locked, and in that moment, I felt an undeniable chemistry that sparked hope deep within.

He was as average-looking as a Latino-Afro-French person could be—which was hot to me. I detected an unassuming presence about him that belied his adventurous spirit. He was an astronaut, after all. His warm, dark eyes held a hint of mischief. Every time that charming smile graced his thick lips, my heart skipped a beat.

With a soft French accent, Wright's voice was a soothing melody that resonated with warmth and authenticity. It was like the gentle lilt of a troubadour's song, filled with tales of far-off places and dreams that reached for the stars. His words flowed effortlessly, painting vivid landscapes of his adventures and aspirations.

I was done.

I knew I had found someone extraordinary. Across the digital divide, our hearts were intertwined, and we committed to each other.

Yet, amidst our digital encounters, I ignored those curious moments when the screen flickered as if refreshing itself. During those fleeting instances, his voice briefly took on an altogether different tone, like a glitch in the seamless connection that bound us. I brushed aside these details, attributing them to the quirks of technology, not realizing its significance in our unfolding story.

As time passed, my longing to meet Wright in person consumed me. I missed him so much. There were so many galaxies between us—he was on a moon beyond any stellar distance I could imagine. Yet, I yearned to touch him. I wanted to feel him in life.

Should I surprise him? Yes!

I decided to spend the little money I had to take a spaceship and land on the place where he'd shared countless stories and dreams—his moon. It was a bold endeavor driven by the madness of my love.

Yes, I was in love with him.

With determination in my heart and a sense of purpose, I embarked on a journey that would bring me closer to Wright than ever before. I was so excited as the lunar surface came into view — where I believed he awaited my arrival.

But when I landed on that desolate lunar landscape, my heart sank. The place was devoid of any signs of life, let alone a man named Wright.

"Are you sure this is the moon he said he was on? People only come here to see where man first landed; they never stay," the ancient pilot of the craft that brought me here asked.

I searched the horizon, desperate for a glimpse of him, but found nothing. It was as if he and the world he had described had vanished into thin air.

Confusion and despair enveloped me. The information he had provided, the coordinates, the descriptions — all were incorrect. The love I had nurtured and the hopes I had cherished shattered like moon dust.

I called him then.

"Wright? Wright! I'm here," I grasped the phone tightly, desperately, as I screamed into it. "Your moon; I'm here! Where are…"

The line went dead.

I tried to reach him, but my calls and messages went unanswered. Wright fell silent, leaving me grappling with the painful truth that the person I had loved might have been fictitious.

Back home, I couldn't bear the weight of unanswered questions and the gaping hole in my heart. I plunged into the digital world, searching every virtual nook and cranny for answers.

I re-read every note we exchanged and watched every recorded interaction I saved through the fog of my sorrow and the mess of my tears.

He had deleted his social media profiles, and all his contact lines and emails were no longer in service or deleted and purged.

Who was Wright? Where had he come from? Why had he disappeared so suddenly? Was he even a natural person or just some sick AI program?

Just when I thought I had reached a dead end, a strange and unsettling revelation emerged from the shadows of the void.

The truth I discovered was not only stranger than I had imagined—and he was closer than I ever would've guessed.

***

Wright

I am right here, Tessa, I thought.

I had watched her since her return from the moon.

She had gone there to meet me in real life, catching me off guard. I wasn't ready for that. I hung up in terror when she called. Then, I disconnected everything and let go of the entire deception.

I had to—I was not the person she wanted me to be, not the elaborate persona I had simulated.

Now, she was trying to find me—the real person behind her dream turned nightmare—the coward who had ghosted her.

Over the past few months, I had roamed the desolate veneer of cyberspace, hiding behind code, seeking solace in staying ahead of the cold cat-and-mouse landscape of her exhaustive online search for her man.

Yet, I was terrified and excited at the prospect of her discovery. Her relentless pursuit unfolded as I stood by the window, watching from two apartments away.

I saw her hunched over her computers, clicking here, there, and everywhere in search of me. I couldn't help but wonder if our reunion would bring me redemption or destruction.

I knew I had to confront her, explain my actions, and reveal the truth about my life and the reasons that had driven me to such drastic measures to get her to fall for me. I hoped she would accept me despite our differences.

I love you, Tessa.

But I was afraid my love would not be enough. I was afraid she would never forgive me when the image she had of me, the dream she had held onto, crumbled away. I had created my avatar, Wright, based on everything I knew she wanted in a man.

I wanted to be everything he was.

Then, I received an unexpected message. It was from her, a simple text in an untraceable chat room I had used only once.

She found me!

Her note read, "I won't stop looking. I need to understand." Her determination was both heartening and terrifying.

Soon after, I decided to make contact, not through the elaborate virtual modes I had used before when I pretended to be Wright.

To man up, I had to discard all the trappings of the modern smoke and mirrors I previously employed to disguise myself.

No, I reached out to her through a simple video call—old school—which would allow me to reveal my true self. I had to be brave.

When she answered, my face was partially obscured in the dimly lit room of my apartment, and her eyes were filled with a mix of anger, hurt, and curiosity.

"Wright? Wright, is that you?"

I was quiet. I was afraid to speak in my natural voice.

She continued, "Why did you run away? Why did you hide yourself from me?" she demanded.

Before I could answer, an emergency vehicle's loud siren pierced the night.

Shoot!

I muted my line too late—she heard the siren in her apartment, its wail slicing through the call that Wright had initiated.

"Wright?" In a whispered, measured tone, she asked, "Where are you right now?"

I was silent for a long beat, the weight of her gaze pressing down on me.

My room was shrouded in darkness, and the silence stretched.

Summoning my resolve, I reached out and clicked on the light on my desk. It hummed to life, illuminating my face with a warm, soft glow.

I looked up slowly, meeting her wide, disbelieving eyes. They were the same eyes that had once looked at me—well, me as her man, Wright—with trust and affection, but now they were filled with shock and confusion.

I saw the recognition consume in her gaze, the moment when my boyish features registered in her mind.

With an astonished tone, she shrieked, "SHELDON!" Her voice pierced the heavy air in the room, and the sound of my real name on her lips felt surreal and painfully ingenuous.

I nodded slowly, unable to find the words to explain and apologize for the disappearance of the person I had pretended to be for months.

She vanished from the screen.

The weight of the ruse and the stress of my deception landed on my chest and exploded out of my eyes in hot tears.

Bang — bang — bang!

***

Tessa

Bang — bang — bang!

My knuckles throbbed with every strike against the door, but the pain barely registered. My whole body trembled with the weight of the truth I had just uncovered. I hit the door again, harder, willing him to answer, to face me.

"Sheldon!" I screamed, my voice tearing through the silence like a collapsing star.

The name felt foreign, wrong, but undeniable. I had called him Wright for months, building him up as someone extraordinary, a man who lived on a distant moon, someone I had thought was waiting for me. But he wasn't real.

He was just a boy — a fifteen-year-old kid fishing me two apartments away!

I stepped back, pressing my palms against my forehead, trying to make sense of the betrayal. How had I been so blind? How could he — a child — be the person I had opened my heart to? He knew what to say and how to present himself as everything I was searching for. But why? Why had he done it?

I pounded the door again, softer this time. The questions swirled, but they tangled in my throat, too tight to scream.

The handle twitched, barely making a sound. Then, with a soft groan, the door inched open, a thin line of light spilling into the hall.

I froze as the light sliced across my skin, my heart slamming against my ribs. And there he was.

Sheldon.

I stood there, locking eyes with him—the boy I'd been chasing across galaxies, across dreams. His eyes were wide with fear, his expression timid, not the confident, adventurous *Wright* I had fallen for. He wasn't what I had imagined. He wasn't anything close. Just a kid standing in the doorway, his expression pale and nervous, his hand clutching the edge of the door.

I swallowed hard, the lump in my throat growing. I felt so stupid, so utterly deceived. I shook as I tried to process how I could have fallen for this.

Tears prickled at my eyes, but I blinked them away, focusing on the reality before me. I looked at him, waiting for him to say something, to explain, but the silence stretched.

And then, as I continued to study him, everything clicked.

Wright had never been real. The gap between us had never been about galaxies or stars or moons—it had always been this—lie.

Tessa, is your love destined to drift aimlessly within this unbridgeable gap, unable to touch him in real life?

That question haunted me again, but this time, I knew the answer. I had wanted something beyond reality, something perfect. And in return, I'd fallen into the suffocating embrace of the lie. This boy, who'd somehow known exactly what I wanted, fed it to me, piece by piece.

I gazed at Sheldon, my anger dissolving into something else.

There were no answers here that could heal the gaping wound in my chest. No explanation that could undo the months I had spent loving someone who didn't exist.

I took one step backward, then another and another— my feet dragging against the floor, burdened by the weight of it all.

Then I turned, straightened my back, and walked with purpose—breaking out of his cosmic gravity and striding into a reality I was determined to make my own.

Love & Marriage

"I Love My Husband, But…"

Miss Shields' modest home smelled faintly of cinnamon and coffee. The sun streamed through half-open blinds, casting slanted rays on the hardwood floor of the living room.

Amy Reis sat upright on the edge of the couch. Her gaze moved from the overflowing bookshelf of worn classics to the family pictures on the mantle. They showed kids with gap-toothed smiles and a man with kind eyes wearing a plain work shirt.

"Thank you for inviting me, Miss Shields," Amy said, smoothing her skirt. Her voice carried the polite stiffness of someone out of their element.

Miss Shields poured coffee into two mismatched mugs, setting one in front of Amy. "Please, call me Cynthia. We're not in school."

Amy smiled and nodded, taking a careful sip of the coffee. It was bitter, but she kept drinking. Miss Shields settled into the armchair across from her, the teacher's familiar authoritative aura softened by the comfort of her own home.

They talked about everything and nothing: poetry and politics, the latest novels, the tediousness of teenage drama.

"I'm going to work at the bank after graduation, Miss Shields. They have already offered me a teller position. I'll save some money and take a year off before I start at the University of the West Indies."

Amy's chest swelled as she outlined her plan. Her eyes gleamed with excitement, and her smile was wide and toothy.

But, Miss Shields leaned forward, eyes sharp and severe now. "Amy, you're brilliant. You have the kind of mind that doesn't come around often, and I want you to hear me on this." She paused, her fingers tracing the rim of her mug. "Go straight to college. Don't take 'a year off' — that year turns into ten before you know it."

Amy nodded, absorbing the weight of her teacher's words.

"Number two," Miss Shields continued, her voice unwavering. "Don't marry until you've achieved all the education you desire. You deserve to focus on yourself first."

Amy's eyes flickered with respect and curiosity as though she saw her teacher in a new light.

"And the third thing," Miss Shields glanced at the photos on the mantle, then back to Amy. "Marry someone on the same economic level as you, or higher. I love my husband, but to take our children to Disney, we must save for years. If we were on the same income level, or if his was higher, things would be different."

Amy didn't speak, just nodded again. The advice felt heavy, as though it was meant to guide her through an invisible maze she couldn't yet see. She glanced at the coffee, then at Miss Shields. The tiny lines at the corners of her teacher's eyes caught her attention.

"I understand," Amy said, and she meant it.

***

Thirty Years Later

Amy stared out the window of her small, well-loved kitchen. The sink was empty, and the clock on the wall ticked steadily. Faint cartoon sounds came from the living room, where her youngest was sprawled on the couch. Her husband, Jim, was hunched over the dining table, scribbling in a notebook. He looked up, offering her a tired smile.

Amy had taken none of Miss Shields' advice.

She'd opted for '*a year off*' that became a decade, then two. At 41, she finally completed her master's degree. She pieced it together through night classes and online courses between shifts and parent-teacher meetings.

She'd married Jim, a man with a high school diploma, just like herself back then. He was kind, steady, reliable. But she was sure this wasn't what Miss Shields had meant. During their marriage, the income gap widened. Jim's job paid what it always had. Amy's degrees raised her salary, but travel was still limited to road trips and camping. The dream vacation to Singapore remained just that—a dream for another year or more.

She loved Jim, no question. He was a good father, her unwavering supporter. But she couldn't shake the quiet, persistent "what if." What if she had followed Miss Shields' advice? What if she had finished school earlier? What if they were on the same financial footing? Would it have made the difference she imagined?

Amy stepped away from the window, picking up a dish towel to dry her hands. She glanced at Jim, now deep in concentration, and she felt the familiar mix of affection and resignation. Life was what it was. She'd chosen this every step of the way. As she watched her husband scribble numbers in his notebook, she heard Miss Shields' clear, confident voice advising her on that long-ago Saturday morning.

"Amy, I love my husband, but...."

***

"I Love My Wife, But..."

Jim was the only Black man in his department and the longest-tenured consultant—and for seven years running, he'd been denied the "Senior" handle. Every performance cycle, he'd watch someone else soar into promotions he'd earned ten times over.

"Jim," John, the department head, said one morning, tapping irritably on a stack of folders, "your execution is rock solid, but these client presentations demand a certain... dynamism. You know what I mean?"

Jim could practically taste the condescension. *Translation: They want a buddy for the clients, someone who greases palms and shares insider jokes at the country club.* He kept his expression neutral. "I'm not sure I follow."

"We value your steady contributions," John continued, "but leadership requires... cultural fit. Perhaps build more camaraderie after hours?"

Right, Jim thought, *because the after-work drinks and golf outings are oh-so-inviting for the lone Black guy who keeps hearing "not a team player" the minute he's not bending over backward.* Today, though, he decided to speak up.

"John, I've delivered on the Grinder, Inc. account for five straight years now. I trained Perry from scratch, and this year he's assigned the lead. But I'm still doing all the operational heavy lifting—"

John raised a hand. "Look, Jim, if you felt overlooked, you should've been more vocal. We can't read minds."

Classic. If he pushed, he was "aggressive"; if he stayed measured, he wasn't "assertive enough." Jim's performance reviews were stuffed with praise—"exceeds expectations" in both the "what" and the "how." Yet promotions slid right past him. He was hitting every target but never hitting the jackpot.

His exasperation escaped in a sigh that felt like a dam giving way. *Enough*, he thought. I'm done playing by rules that never change.

He turned away and returned to his desk. Early that evening, as he locked up his drawers, the metal sliders groaned almost in sympathy with the invisible ceiling he'd been battered against for years. John didn't toss any last-minute "emergency" audits at him this time — probably too busy ignoring Jim's existence after that conversation. Normally, it was "Jim, buddy, can you handle this before tomorrow's meeting?" at five past closing.

Clearing his inbox felt strangely hollow. Everything was done, but the real issue remained: the system refused to let him rise. Another sigh, but he barely noticed it. They'd become a reflex, a kind of punctuation in his days. He knew it was time to go home, but a knot of tension weighed on his chest, the same knot that had him fantasizing about turning in a leave-of-absence form for that three-week escape Amy had been hinting at since forever. Of course, John would probably spin that as "lack of commitment."

Shrugging on his coat, Jim adjusted the tie he insisted on wearing daily. In the post-pandemic world, the entire office — especially guys like Perry — had settled into a permanent uniform of chinos and open collars. But Jim believed in showing up with excellence, whether or not anyone noticed.

On his way out, he caught his reflection in the restroom mirror: honey-brown skin under the fluorescent glare, eyes ringed with tired shadows. The lines of his jacket were still crisp, as if he were trying to starch away the feeling of unraveling inside. The difference between him and everyone else might've been subtle, but it was there. He was the guy who showed up polished and stayed invisible anyway.

His coworkers had never seen the Jim who dominated the monthly domino games at his house, the one who cracked jokes so funny that drinks ended up on the floor. In the basement, trash talk flew, kids called him Uncle Jim, and friends teased him for nailing a perfect Trinidadian accent when he impersonated his mother-in-law. That Jim didn't exist from nine to five.

With a final exhale, he left for Grand Central. He moved slower than usual through the sea of pinstriped suits and stiff shoulders. Each commuter wore the same harried mask. They bustled in unison, a massive machine of human cogs. Sometimes he wondered if any of them ever felt like him—restless to be seen, but afraid to rock the boat.

He let two trains pass, drifting through the cavernous station, eyes on the cosmic mural overhead. When he finally boarded, he chose a corner seat in a half-empty car. *Maybe I'll tell Amy that Perry had dumped a project on me again.* She'd see right through that, as always, but at least she'd understand the weight of being "Reliable Jim."

City lights blurred outside. In his reflection, he caught the shape of a man with perfect posture, perfect tie, and a desperate look in his eyes. That silent cry nearly made him turn away.

"Excuse me."

He glanced up. A striking woman with elegant locs and a confident smile stood before him. Her tailored blazer suggested she knew the corporate game too, though her blouse, hugging her curves, hinted she wasn't afraid to be noticed. He felt an unexpected jolt, like he'd been nudged awake.

"Is this seat taken?" she asked, her gaze drifting to the spot beside him, then back to lock with his.

He shifted. "It's all yours."

As she settled, her perfume—spicy, jasmine undertones—cocooned them in an intimate corner of the train. A sudden heat rose in Jim's chest. It felt good to be seen, even by a stranger.

"Tough day?" She nodded at his loosened tie.

Jim actually laughed. "That obvious?"

"Please. I've worked in corporate America long enough to spot the dignified exhaustion. I'm Naomi."

"Jim." He met her eyes and found himself smiling back. Something about her directness cracked his usual guarded shell. "Headed to West Haven."

"Milford for me. Next stop, actually." She paused, a playful flicker in her gaze. "Unless I decide to ride further."

A small bump on the track pressed their shoulders together for a moment, and Jim felt a swirl of attraction—and a reminder of everything he'd set aside for the sake of stability. He pictured himself following Naomi off the train, trading war stories over whiskey in some hidden bar, letting the rest of the night unfold without obligations. For once, letting life happen.

She must've sensed it. "Ever tempted to get off at a different stop?"

He turned the question over in his mind, letting it sink past his corporate persona. "I used to think about different stops all the time. Different lives." He paused. "Now…I'm learning to appreciate the one I chose."

Naomi's smile was kind. "I can respect that."

The train slowed. Her stop. She got up and adjusted her bag, but then pivoted before stepping off. "Whoever it is that put that shadow in your eyes—they don't deserve you." And then she was gone, a swirl of perfume and possibility left in her wake.

Jim watched the platform recede. Naomi had stirred something in him, but it wasn't just lust. It was a longing for change, a reminder that it was still possible to break the script. Maybe he could request that time off, force the higher-ups to manage without him for a few weeks. Maybe, just maybe, they'd realize how much they relied on Jim.

But he knew that world too well. Rocking the boat could cost everything.

When the train reached West Haven, he merged with the quiet exodus toward the parking lot, found his old 1999 Audi, and navigated the rows of uniform houses until he reached his. The porch light illuminated Amy's flowers. She'd be inside, probably checking a student's essay at the kitchen table, a symphony of pots simmering on the stove behind her. He lingered in the car, shoulders heavy.

He remembered Mr. Knight from high school, pacing the art room, giddy with praise over one of Jim's surrealist oils. "You've got the spark," Mr. Knight had told him. "This could hang in a gallery. Don't waste your gift, Jim." But reality had overshadowed that dream—college bills, family obligations, no safety net.

Jim let the engine idle another minute. He'd done what he had to: marry young when Amy got pregnant, take that first accounting job to pay for diapers. He might never have chosen the corporate world otherwise. Still, he'd built a good life here, a stable one, with a wife he loved and two kids who were thriving. He was proud. But some piece of him—maybe the artist—was adrift, wondering if it was too late to want more.

Finally, he stepped into the house. The smell of onions and garlic confirmed dinner was nearly done. Amy sat at the table, piles of essays and a red pen in hand. She didn't look up immediately.

"You're late," she said, scribbling a comment in the margin.

"John's brand of drama." He hung up his coat. "Perry needed me to 'fix' his numbers again."

Amy snorted softly. "And no doubt he'll be the hero in tomorrow's meeting?"

Jim shrugged. "He usually is."

She glanced up, eyes lingering a second longer than usual. "Uh-huh."

Jim knew she saw more than he voiced. She had a knack for that—reading the silent tension in his posture. But he wasn't ready to rehash his day. "How was yours?" he asked, dropping into a chair.

She pushed her glasses higher. "Busy, but good. I've got one student who's an incredible writer. But her parents think it's a waste of time, keep pushing her toward 'practical' stuff." Amy sighed. "She's losing that spark."

Something clenched in Jim's chest. He sipped the water she'd placed out for him—like she always did, without fail. "That's tough," he said quietly.

Amy looked at him more closely. "You okay?"

He mustered a small smile. "Sure. Just…long day."

A flicker of concern crossed her face, but she just nodded. "You're working too hard. We both know that."

"Somebody's gotta keep the lights on," he said lightly, though the words felt heavier than he intended. Standing, he moved to the fridge but paused with his hand on the door. "You know," he said, turning around, "I've been thinking about taking some time off. Like… that trip you always talk about."

Amy set her pen down. "Trip?"

"Singapore?" He tried to sound casual, though the idea had been burning in him since Naomi's mention of different stops. "The one you've been daydreaming about for years—sipping cocktails by that infinity pool you keep showing me on your phone."

Amy's eyebrows shot up. "You? Seriously?" She stared as though she couldn't decide if he was joking.

Jim walked back to the table, lowering himself into the chair across from her. "Yeah. Seriously. I need a break."

He almost expected her to tease him, but instead, she leaned forward, eyes full of worry and hope at once. "Jim, that would be… I mean, we've talked about it forever. What's changed?"

His lips curled into a half-smile. "I'm just tired of living on autopilot. Maybe it's time to choose something else."

For a heartbeat, they just stared at each other. Then Amy's mouth curved into a genuine, bright smile that reminded him of her carnival-queen laughter back in the day. "Yes. Let's do it."

His chest loosened, as if he'd been holding his breath for years.

They set the table together, but Jim's mind already spun with the possibility of telling John he was taking a real vacation. The next morning, he planned to do just that.

***

Jim's plan hit a snag immediately. At nine sharp, he stepped into John's office, summoning every ounce of calm.

34

"Time off?" John frowned, pushing his wire-rim glasses higher on his nose. "For three weeks, Jim?"

Jim fought the tightening in his gut. "Yes, I have a lot of PTO accrued. And I'd appreciate your approval."

John leaned back, steepling his fingers. "Well, you know how valuable you are, especially in Q2. We're slammed with audits. Perry's still ramping up on the new accounts."

"I'm aware. But I've got everything documented. I can hand off tasks—"

"You might want to reconsider the timing," John said, a vague paternal note in his voice that set Jim's teeth on edge. "I'm not sure taking an extended vacation right now demonstrates senior leadership potential."

Jim inhaled slowly. There it was, the veiled threat that if he dared prioritize himself, he'd lose any chance at "Senior Consultant." The game never changed.

"I hear you," Jim said, schooling his face into neutrality. "But I do have the time, and I've been handling more than my share. I'm taking the trip."

John's lips thinned. "I see. Let's talk about it in a couple of days. I need to look at the pipeline."

Pushed aside, like always. Jim gave a polite nod and left, anger thrumming in his veins. Sure enough, by 5:15 p.m., an "urgent request" from John landed on Jim's desk—some incomplete data sets that Perry had flubbed.

***

The next day, Perry leaned over Jim's cubicle with a smirk. "Hey man, I really appreciate you cleaning up that data. You know, leadership's noticing how we pull together as a team."

"Sure," Jim said, refusing to look up from the spreadsheet. He was half-tempted to drop a random formula error in there and let Perry deal with the fallout, but that wasn't who he was. He breathed through the impulse. "Anything else?"

"Actually," Perry said, lowering his voice conspiratorially, "John's inviting a few of us to an evening golf clinic. Some big client's CFO will be there. Networking opportunity." He shrugged as if it was no big deal. "I mean, maybe you could stop by if you want."

Jim looked up, scanning Perry's face for sincerity. He got the sense Perry was only mentioning it as an afterthought, maybe because John told him to. "Yeah, right. Thanks for letting me know. Short notice, though."

"It's tonight," Perry said, fiddling with the file in his hands. "At the West Ridge Country Club. You any good at golf?"

Jim forced a laugh. "I dabble." That was half-true; he'd once tried to learn, but the subtle signals from his colleagues back then had made it clear he wasn't entirely welcome. Jokes about his swing, his stance—harmless on the surface, but always tinged with something else.

"Cool, see you there if you can make it." Perry flashed a grin and strolled off, leaving Jim with a simmering frustration. The invitation didn't feel real. More like a test: Show up and be the "team player," or skip and confirm he didn't have the "right fit."

He texted Amy:

They want me at some golf thing tonight. Could be an in with a big client.

Her response came quickly:

Go. Show them who you are. We can talk Singapore after. Good luck.

He smiled despite himself. Amy always believed in him, even when he struggled to believe in himself.

***

Sunset painted the sky in pink and gold as Jim arrived at West Ridge Country Club. Lush fairways spread out under bright floodlights, and the parking lot gleamed with BMWs and Teslas. He found John, Perry, and a few others in pressed polos, casual but expensive. They gave him polite smiles.

"Glad you could make it, Jim," John said, though his voice lacked genuine warmth. "Let's tee off, see how you do."

Jim forced a grin. "Sure thing."

The CFO they were courting, a silver-haired man named Bennett, wore an effortless smile as he bantered with John and Perry about stock portfolios. Jim tried to insert a comment about the changing markets, but the conversation glided right over him. It was as though he'd never opened his mouth.

When they reached the practice range, John handed out clubs. Jim took a practice swing, carefully aligning his posture. He was no pro, but he could hold his own.

Bennett watched Jim's first swing land decently on the green. "Not bad," he said, eyebrows raised. "You play often?"

"Now and then," Jim replied. "I'm better at spreadsheets than swings, honestly."

That earned him a short laugh from Bennett—but John quickly redirected the talk back to the CFO's upcoming investment strategy. Jim was left standing in the background, feeling like an accessory.

At one point, Perry jogged over, feigning camaraderie. "Jim, we might need your help with those numbers for the CFO's pitch deck. I told him you're the best at analyzing risk profiles."

"Oh?" Bennett turned. "You're the risk guru?"

Jim smiled tightly. "I handle a lot of the operational and analytical side. Yes."

"Perry's taught me plenty," Bennett said, nodding at Perry.

Taught him? Jim had to swallow the retort. He offered a forced smile and let it go. It was the usual routine: Jim's contributions being fed to a higher-up as though Perry was the mastermind.

As the evening wore on, a pit of disappointment formed in Jim's stomach. He'd shown up, hoping to prove he could fit into their world, but it was as if they had a script in mind — Perry and John as the frontmen, Jim an afterthought. *So much for "cultural fit."*

By the time the final balls were driven, Jim felt more drained than ever. He excused himself, claiming an early morning. John barely acknowledged his departure, too busy laughing with Bennett and congratulating Perry on a "stellar swing."

***

It was nearly nine when Jim reached his car. He sat in the driver's seat for a few seconds, letting the quiet envelop him. He couldn't keep doing this. Naomi's question echoed: *Ever tempted to get off at a different stop?*

The truth was, yes, he was. Desperately.

He thought of Amy's expression when he'd mentioned Singapore. He thought of Jas, who still needed to see his dad living, not just existing. Janet was off to college — did he want her to think this was all adult life had to offer?

He started the engine, determination coiling inside him. The next time he talked to John, he'd make it clear: he was taking his vacation, period. If that blew up his shot at "Senior Consultant," so be it. What had that shot gotten him anyway?

***

On the drive home, a memory of his teenage self rose unbidden. He and Amy were nineteen, at a backyard barbecue in Queens. The sun was blazing, the air thick with the scent of jerk chicken and the bass of soca music pounding from the speakers. Amy, in denim shorts and a halter top, laughed with her cousins. He'd felt like the luckiest man in the world.

His mother had pulled him aside, a rare worried look in her tired eyes. "You sure you ready for this, son? A baby changes everything."

"I'm sure," he'd said, voice trembling. "I love her."

His mother sighed. "Just make sure you don't end up like your father — starting a family you can't provide for."

The words cut deep, but they forged a vow in him that day. He'd never walk out on his responsibilities. He'd choose security for the people he loved, no matter what it cost him personally.

He flicked on his headlights, that vow echoing with both pride and sorrow. Now, after all this time, he was learning there was a difference between providing and living.

***

Back in the kitchen, Amy was scrubbing a pot, the house otherwise quiet. Jas had likely gone to bed. Jim set his keys on the counter.

She glanced over her shoulder, turning off the tap. "So, how was it?"

Jim shrugged off his jacket, rolling his neck to ease the tension. "As expected. Perry talked. John bragged. I was basically a prop."

Amy dried her hands, a sympathetic look in her eyes. "I'm sorry."

"It's fine." He took a breath, remembering the swirl of the evening, the invisible lines dividing who belonged and who was allowed to speak. "Listen, about the leave— I asked John. He gave me the usual runaround, said we'd 'discuss' it in a few days."

Amy's shoulders tensed, but she forced a small smile. "Then we keep pushing." Her voice softened. "Jim, this means a lot to me—to us. I can handle a wait, but we need to do this."

He closed the distance between them and gently touched her arm. "I know. And we will. I promise."

Her eyes locked onto his. "Don't let them talk you out of it."

That flicker of steel in her tone was one of the reasons he'd fallen for her in the first place. "I won't."

She nodded, relaxing. "Okay. Let's go to bed. We can figure out the details tomorrow."

Jim squeezed her hand, a grateful warmth filling him. Together, they'd stand their ground.

***

The following week crawled by. John kept putting Jim off, day after day, citing "urgent client matters." Meanwhile, the tension in the office mounted as the CFO from the golf outing moved forward with a major account. Perry paraded around like he was the newly minted star.

Late Thursday, well after the office had emptied, John finally summoned Jim. "Let's chat about your leave," he said, not bothering to hide his exasperation. "Close the door."

Jim stepped inside and shut it, steeling himself.

John folded his hands on the desk. "Look, this new account is a huge opportunity for us. It's all hands on deck. Perry's good, but he still leans on you. So here's what I propose: hold off on your leave for now, help us establish a strong foundation, and we'll reassess in a few months."

Jim blinked. "A few months?"

"Jim, I'm trying to be fair. You're vital. But if you vanish for three weeks now, it sends the wrong message. Especially since we're considering the Senior Consultant role. Show us your commitment, and we'll show you ours."

Silence thickened in the room. Jim's eyes fell on the plaque behind John's head that read, "Teamwork Makes the Dream Work." The irony made him want to laugh. For years, he'd been a team of one, carrying the weight of a department that refused to see him as a leader. Now, they expected him to surrender his own well-being yet again for a carrot that never materialized.

"No," Jim said, voice surprisingly calm.

John looked startled. "Excuse me?"

"I said no. I'm taking my vacation. I've earned it, and I'm giving you notice."

John's brow furrowed. "If you do this, Jim, I can't guarantee—"

"You never guaranteed anything," Jim cut in, voice still measured. He stood. "If that jeopardizes my shot at the title, so be it. Because I'm starting to think I've been chasing a ghost."

A flicker of something—anger, or perhaps disbelief—flashed across John's face. "You realize this could harm your future here."

Jim nodded. "I do. I'm still going."

John looked away, and for the first time, he didn't have a pat response. Jim turned and walked out, an odd mixture of fear and relief beating in his chest. For once, he wasn't letting them dictate his life.

***

In the days that followed, Jim began delegating tasks to Perry—gently but firmly. If Perry was the star, let him handle the show. John avoided him, probably hoping Jim would crack and rescind his request.

At night, Jim and Amy pored over travel sites, beaming at photos of Singapore's modern skyline, the vibrant hawker centers, the iconic Marina Bay Sands. Jas hovered, enthralled by images of futuristic architecture, while Janet chimed in via group chat from college, excited to join the trip if her schedule allowed.

One evening, as Amy finalized reservations, Jim found himself rummaging in a dusty box in the basement. Amid old notebooks and junk, he discovered a sketchpad from high school. The corners were worn, but inside were half-finished sketches—a few surreal cityscapes, swirling with color. His breath caught at the forgotten passion on those pages.

He spread them on the basement floor, feeling the old hunger to create again. He tested a pencil on yellowed paper. Just a quick line turned into shading, which turned into form. Time slid by in quiet fascination until he heard the basement steps creak.

Amy peeked her head in. "What are you up to?"

Jim glanced up, sheepish. "Just found these old sketches. From when I thought I might be an artist."

She came closer, crouching beside him. "Might be? You clearly are one."

He exhaled. "I was, maybe."

Amy placed a hand on his shoulder. "You are," she repeated gently. Then she kissed his temple. "I always wondered if you'd pick this up again."

"I almost forgot how good it feels," he admitted, gaze drifting over the shapes. "It's like... part of me has been asleep."

She squeezed his shoulder. "Maybe your vacation can be about more than rest. Maybe it's about rediscovering yourself."

He looked at her, emotions tangled in his chest. "I love you," he whispered.

She smiled that bright, confident smile that first won him over. "I know. And I love you enough to want you whole."

***

Two weeks later, Jim and Amy stood in the airport terminal, waiting for their flight to Singapore. Jas buzzed with excitement, exploring every corner of the waiting area. Janet had managed to take a short break from summer classes to join them, grinning as she scrolled through possible excursions they could try.

Jim's phone vibrated. He glanced at it: a message from Perry.

We're drowning here. John's losing it. Could really use your expertise on the CFO's project.

Then, a second text:

Please?

Jim inhaled. Amy, noticing his expression, rubbed his back gently. "Everything okay?"

He showed her the messages, a rueful smirk on his face. "They need me, apparently."

"Yeah, they do," Amy said. "But do you need them right now?"

He looked around at his family, all of them brimming with anticipation. "No," he said softly, typing back a single line:

Sorry, on vacation.

He powered off the phone, slid it into his pocket.

For a moment, a pang of fear trembled through him — fear of what might happen to his career. But there was also a swelling sense of freedom. He had chosen this stop, at least for now.

***

We Love Each Other, And...

They watched the sun dip behind the Singapore skyline from the rooftop of Marina Bay Sands, the neon glow dancing on the infinity pool's surface. Amy let her gaze drift to Jas and Janet, splashing at the edge, trying (and failing) to appear nonchalant as they snapped selfies. Watching her teenage son and college-age daughter soaking in such a lavish experience felt surreal. Back home, the budget always seemed tight, but here, for a few precious weeks, they'd tasted freedom from routine.

For Jim, the trip had been a revelation — a chance to step off the corporate hamster wheel and breathe. He still remembered the look of shock on John's face when he announced he was taking his PTO, no matter how "inconvenient" the timing. Now, with a golden sunset haloing the Singapore skyline, Jim felt more like himself than he had in years.

Amy floated closer, recalling Miss Shields' advice — graduate first, marry someone with equal or greater means, always stay on firm financial footing. None of that had gone to plan. Instead, she'd taken the scenic route through night classes, motherhood, and a marriage that was both anchor and sail. But here they were, side by side, children laughing, hearts light. Sometimes, the best script is the one you write yourself.

A week later, all four of them sprawled on the living-room sofa, flipping through photos. Janet teased Jas about his sloppy attempts at hawker-center delicacies while Jim recounted how he nearly fell into the pool taking a panoramic shot. Amy listened, half-lost in her own joy at seeing them all so relaxed.

Then Jim's phone buzzed: an email from John. The subject line read, "Restructuring Announcement — Next Steps." A hush settled. Jim stared at the screen without tapping it, a dull thud in his chest. Did it signal new opportunities or fresh obstacles? After a moment, he set the phone aside.

"Later." His hand found Amy's, and he glanced around at his family. "Whatever it is can wait."

Scarlet Ibis James

48

Seven Was the Symbol of Their Love

Nancy—her heritage reflected in her honeyed onyx skin—and Bill, fair and freckled, crossed paths at a party neither had planned to attend. She was there because her friend insisted, and he tagged along because his buddy promised laughs and no expectations.

Within the first hour, they gravitated to the kitchen, both reaching for the same bottle of wine. Their laughter flowed as naturally as the pinot, and by night's end, Bill found himself planning their second date without even asking if she was free.

***

Two weeks later—after a blur of quick discourse and quicker intimacy—they were wed in a state building that smelled of cold marble and bureaucracy. Nancy wasn't interested in a church wedding; Bill was, but he tucked that wish away alongside the simple white gold band he slid onto her finger.

***

Seven days in, their first quarrel erupted over a missing mug—her favorite, a gift from a friend so distant she supposedly couldn't recall the name. Bill's eyes flashed with something unrecognizable, a fleeting spark of anger or uncertainty. By Saturday, the mug mysteriously reappeared, tension briefly forgotten—though neither would speak of why.

***

Seven months later, Nancy was fastening her earring in the bedroom. "Bill, are you ready? We're already late," she called out.

He stood in the kitchen, staring at a mug of coffee gone cold. "Do we have to go?" he asked quietly, the fridge's hum threatening to swallow the words.

Nancy appeared in the doorway, her brow creased. "I told them we'd be there. It's just brunch."

Bill ran a hand through his hair. "I know, but it's been a long week. Maybe we could just…stay in? You and me?"

She sighed, feeling the weight of his hesitation. "I understand you're tired, but these are my friends. We barely see them anymore."

His silence spoke volumes, and her posture stiffened. "Fine. Stay. Have your coffee."

He set the mug down with a louder-than-intended clink. "I'll come. Just…give me a minute." Their eyes locked in a silent standoff before Nancy turned and walked away. Bill watched her retreating back with a growing ache that said it shouldn't be this difficult so soon.

***

By their seventh year, Nancy had grown used to Bill's unspoken disappointments. She filled her life with new hobbies and fresh faces from her diaspora—always pressing forward as if she feared standing still. Bill watched, half-proud and half-lonely, never giving voice to his unease.

***

They commemorated that seventh anniversary with a quiet dinner, a nod to their beginnings but stripped of the early heat. Over dessert, they laughed about their first fight, the long-since-replaced mug an odd symbol for something neither could name. Only, she did name something else…

"Kwame."

"What?"

"The mug. It was a gift from my first boyfriend, Kwame."

***

Twenty-one months later, they found themselves in a lawyer's office, divorce papers spread across the table. Everything between them lay there—unraveled in slow motion, transcribed in legal language that seemed both blunt and surreal.

"So, this is it?" Bill asked, as though searching for Nancy to contradict him.

"Yeah," she said softly, her gaze fixed on the pen in her hand. "It's time."

He leaned back, running his thumb along the edge of the table. "I really thought we'd make it to ten."

Nancy inhaled, steadying her thoughts, and signed her name. The pen hovered a moment too long, as if hesitating. Finally, she looked up. "Ten wasn't our number."

They exchanged final signatures in silence, each stroke a small, irrevocable step away from what they had once promised.

Outside, sunlight blazed in stark contrast to the somber mood. Nancy paused on the sidewalk, offering Bill a tight-lipped smile that conveyed both gratitude and regret. Then she turned and walked away.

Bill watched her figure recede into the brightness. Yes, he thought. She was right. Seven was always our number.

We Couldn't Then, But We Can Now

What is it about the things we don't say? The missed moments, the glances exchanged but never acted upon. Do they vanish with time or linger, waiting for the right moment to resurface?

I hadn't thought about him in years. But as I stood at the corner of Main and West in Annapolis, waiting for the light to change, I realized the memory hadn't faded. It hovered there, tugging at me.

At that moment, I remembered that I had been at a conference in Maryland. It was a sprawling corporate event where everyone looked polished and spoke with rehearsed confidence.

I was a presenter leading a panel on international business strategies for emerging markets. I loved being a Black woman executive who impressed everyone. My presentation had been a success, the kind that left me buzzing, ready for the next challenge.

He had been there, too, leading a discussion on logistics in global trade. His deep and confident voice turned many heads in the crowded room. He wore his ambition on his aura. That, his icy blue eyes, chestnut brown hair, and spectacular smile certainly turned my head.

Jakub.

During his panel discussion, our eyes locked for a few moments too long. Something in his lingering gaze — curiosity, heat — caught me. It was just a flash, but enough to lodge an idea in my mind of what could be. It was the first time I ever felt anything like that. It was as if something came alive in me when he looked at me.

Later, I found myself at my company's booth, handing out brochures and business cards and conversing politely with potential clients. I half-expected — hoped — Jakub would pass by, maybe stop, introduce himself. But he didn't. The hours wore on, and as the crowds thinned, I realized he wasn't coming. Disappointment? Perhaps, but I refused to entertain the feelings.

That night, I went home to Nuru, my husband, my Black king, and buried the memory of the gorgeous White man under the weight of work and love. My husband was from my community. We had grown up together and we made sense. Although passion and desire were never present, I did not believe I needed those things to be happy. Nuru's kind smile and his patient heart always kept me grounded.

But life, with its cruel timing, unraveled our plans. His battle with prostate cancer was swift and relentless. When it took him, it left a hollow ache in my chest that no amount of professional success could fill — not immediately, anyway.

I threw myself into work — travel, contracts, boardrooms. It was more convenient to maintain some distance from everyone. I became Georgieta Koroma — widow, businesswoman, unflinchingly independent. But now, standing in front of a grocery store in Maryland, where that conference had taken place, the memory resurfaced. I hadn't expected to think about him again, much less see him.

Inside, the store was nearly empty — perfect. I wasn't in the mood for people. I made my way to the wine aisle, my fingers grazing the neck of a bottle when I heard it.

"Georgieta?"

That voice — deep, obviously Polish accent — sent a shiver down my spine. I recognized it without needing to turn. Did I manifest him? Slowly, I released the bottle and faced him.

Jakub Lewandowski.

The years had been kind to him. His hair was streaked with silver now, but it suited him. He still stood tall, broad-shouldered, commanding attention without seeming to try. His eyes, the same pale blue I remembered, held mine with an intensity that stirred something primal inside me, different from the feelings I felt for Nuru.

"Jakub," I said, the name strange yet sweet on my tongue, like strawberries and cottage cheese. "You remember me?"

"I do," he nodded, his voice carrying that rich timbre like dark honey, smooth and warm. "I didn't think I'd ever see you again."

I offered a small smile, struggling to keep my voice steady. "Life happens, doesn't it?"

He chuckled softly, but his gaze was intense. "It does. But I must admit, I asked around about you back then. Tried to find out who you were."

That surprised me. "You did?"

"Yeah," he nodded, looking almost sheepish. "I saw you at your booth. You seemed… out of my league."

I raised an eyebrow. "Out of your league?"

He laughed, glancing away momentarily before his eyes found mine again.

"You were… impressive. Too much for me, maybe."

I tilted my head, curious now. "You didn't seem like a man who would let intimidation get in his way."

He let out a breath, rubbing the back of his neck. "It wasn't just that. I was married. My wife, Magda. So whatever spark I might've felt… I couldn't act on it."

The honesty caught me off guard — no apology, just the plain truth of why he'd kept his distance. I respected it, though it added a new complexity to what we'd shared.

"You felt a spark?" I asked, my voice soft.

His grin widened, a little shy, a little bold. "Yeah, I did. It confused me, to be honest. I've never experienced anything like that before or since. Well… until right now."

I nodded, letting the moment settle. "I understand."

For a moment, neither of us spoke, the weight of his confession lingering between us.

"Coffee?" he asked. "Catch up?"

I hesitated. The instinct to protect myself, to keep my walls up, tugged at me, but something softer, quieter urged me forward.

"Okay," I said, the decision loosening a knot inside me. "Coffee."

***

The café was tucked between a row of shops that had long since closed for the night. It wasn't the kind of place with soft lighting and jazz but rather the kind where night owls and late-shift workers go for strong coffee and a quick meal. The background conversation was muffled, a steady undercurrent beneath the fluorescent buzz.

Jakub found a booth by the window, and I slid in across from him. The space between us felt both comfortable and uncertain.

He ordered black coffee for both of us, and I let him, not because I needed him to, but because it felt easy.

We started with small talk—work, travel, the usual— but it wasn't long before the conversation deepened.

"I remember you worked for a big firm back then," Jakub said, "Are you still with them?"

"No, I started my own practice a few years ago. We're doing quite well."

He tented his eyebrows. "Wow, that was a bold decision. A woman starting a tech consultancy is not traditional. Why did you decide to do that?"

I leaned back, considering my answer. "Necessity, I suppose. After Nuru…passed, I needed something to throw myself into. Building my own company gave me that."

He nodded slowly, his gaze thoughtful. "I get that. After Magda died, work was all I had."

I hadn't known about Magda, but hearing him say her name eased something between us. We both carried loss. We didn't need to explain it — it was there, understood.

"I'm sorry," I said quietly.

"Thank you," he replied, his voice soft. "It was hard for a long time. But, like you, work gave me something to focus on."

We sat in silence for a moment, letting the weight of our shared grief settle. It wasn't uncomfortable. It felt necessary.

"I didn't expect this," I admitted, cracking the quiet open. "Running into you after all these years."

"Neither did I," he smiled. "But maybe that's a good thing. Sometimes the best things happen when we're not looking for them."

***

After that café reunion, we fell into a rhythm. Jakub lived in Annapolis, and I lived in Oakland. Our lives were well established, and neither of us wanted to uproot ourselves. But there was something between us — a connection we didn't want to let slip away.

One evening, as we sat in my apartment, both of us quieter than usual, Jakub spoke.

"So, how do we make this work?" he asked, his fingers tracing the rim of his coffee cup.

I took a breath, looking at his hands, leaning into the question. "We keep our lives, our routines. But we choose each other."

A slow smile spread across his face. "I like that. We don't have to change everything. We just have to show up."

"Yes," I said, feeling the truth of it. "We don't have to lose ourselves."

***

We gradually found our relationship's edges and its center. We fell into a groove — phone calls after work, long weekends together, small moments when time allowed and even a vacation together in Uganda. We didn't make grand sacrifices or drastic moves. We let things be, for the most part.

But it wasn't all easy. There were moments when Jakub's alpha male tendencies clashed with my sense of autonomy. He liked to take charge and be in control. At times, this grated on me. I had fought hard for my success and agency, and I wasn't about to let anyone take that away from me.

One evening, after a particularly heated argument, I confronted him.

"You didn't even ask me, Jakub!" I seethed, crossing my arms. "How could you assume you know what the best layout of my home office should be and approve plans to begin the work."

He straightened, a look of surprise in his eyes, and for a moment, neither of us spoke.

"You don't always have to be in control, Jakub," I said. "I'm not some damsel in distress who needs saving."

He looked taken aback a moment longer, then nodded slowly. "I know. I'm sorry. It's just... how I've always been."

"I'm not asking you to change who you are," I said, softening my tone. "But you need to understand that I'm not the type of woman who will be overshadowed."

Jakub was silent, then he sighed, running a hand through his hair. "You're right. I'm used to being the strong one, the one who takes care of things. But I see now that I don't always have to be that way with you. You are strong too."

I nodded, feeling a sense of relief wash over me. "Exactly."

Jakub was as confident as ever but didn't try to take control. He listened and allowed me space, and in return, I learned to lean on him when it felt right. There continued to be moments when his assertiveness clashed with my independence, but we worked through them. We respected each other's need for autonomy.

***

We continued to learn how to be with one another.

In the quiet moments, over shared cups of coffee or glasses of wine, I realized we had found a version of love that fit us. We were equals — independent yet deeply connected, choosing each other when it mattered most.

Eventually, I admitted, "I love you."

I'd wanted to say this to Jakub for months, but I was afraid of how he would take it. *Would it scare him off? Would it scare me off?*

But the words flowed from my lips like a rich, savory broth—warming, unexpected, and deeply satisfying. And the good feeling rose even more when he responded.

"I'm in love with you." He declared it in a rush, as if he, too, had been simmering with those feelings for longer than he cared to admit.

Scarlet Ibis James

What is it about the things we don't say? The missed chances? I realized they don't vanish. They become part of us, imprinted on our souls, waiting for the right time to reappear.

"We did not have perfect timing, but we had the grace of a second chance," I said.

"We couldn't then, but we can now."

Behind the Grand Doors of Paradise

Why did Cleolin, with her stunning eyes and captivating smile, wield the power to illuminate and complicate my world? This was the question that had infected Carlos' thoughts that very morning.

He stood here, on the edge of Harlem, where the city's ceaseless energy collided with the tranquil aura of Columbia University's campus. He stood sentinel in the lobby of the modest yet elegant Paradise building, where a seamless blend of old-world charm and modern sophistication whispered tales of the past.

Mahogany wood adorned the walls, while vintage chandeliers cast a warm, nostalgic glow over the polished marble floors. Now collecting dust, a grand piano stood as a silent testament to the building's rich jazz history.

Carlos often wondered if he had disappointed his ancestors, his life tethered to the role of a doorman in this aging, no-longer-a-skyscraper edifice. As a second-generation

Filipino-American, he observed the building's residents pass by, their lives seemingly disconnected from his own.

In his crisp uniform, behind his plastered-on, seemingly genuine smile, Carlos oscillated between love and hate for his job. This dichotomy chained him to the stability of an income while constantly reminding him of the dreams that had eluded him.

This morning, soft New York City light bathed the lobby as the residents started their daily routines. Between 7:00 and 8:30, Carlos conjured up snippets of stories about three of the building's inhabitants as they ventured out to face their shiny world.

First was Mrs. Fitzgerald, a graceful woman in her forties who was working as an art curator. Carlos imagined her meticulously arranging paintings and sculptures, injecting life into art he secretly despised.

Next was Mr. Johnson, a no-nonsense lawyer perpetually in a rush. Carlos pictured him as a fearless courtroom warrior, battling for justice in the concrete jungle. The irony didn't escape him; his life often felt like an unending skirmish against the mundane, an uncelebrated hero guarding Paradise's gates.

Then there was Sar'aah, a young, aspiring actress whose dreams seemed to permeate the building's atmosphere as she moved through it. He envisioned her attending auditions and not captivating casting directors with her talent, so she returns home later in the day, disheartened and detached after a string of rejections and no callbacks.

He thought matter-of-factly, She is squandering her parents' money on this overpriced apartment.

Amid these musings, one tenant occupied his thoughts more than others — Cleolin from apartment 5F. He thought of her eyes, deep pools of mystery harboring the secrets of a thousand stories; he was sure. Her radiant and infectious smile brightened his day whenever it graced his vision.

Interrupting his daydream, a delivery person arrived at 10:43 with a stack of groceries. Carlos acknowledged the young, very dark-skinned African with a polite nod. Yet, he couldn't help but ponder the residents' culinary preferences and the stories concealed within those grocery bags.

Does Cleolin cook Adobo? I want to teach her how to make it, to share that savory and flavorful Filipino dish with her, he mused. Ah, Cleolin.

Cleolin — her graceful walk was like a dance through life's challenges, an effortless dignity he admired. Yet, there were thoughts he dared not admit — the softness of her voice, the warmth of her laughter, the comforting aura of her presence.

It was clear Carlos was infatuated with Cleolin but understood it was an unspoken yearning that could never be acted upon.

He shook his head, trying to banish the thought of her to the recesses of his mind.

The day unfolded with routine precision until 11:53, when another delivery person arrived. This time, lunch from an overpriced salad bar was destined for a tall, *malaki*, single Black woman working from home. She had wild hair, even wilder clothing styles and lived on the 9th floor. Carlos imagined her seated by a window, engrossed in her laptop, the city's frenzied life outside serving as both distraction and muse.

What does she do for a living? He wondered.

Then, Cleolin appeared outside the glass doors of Paradise.

Her presence cast a spell over the surroundings as she approached the entrance. Carlos' mind went blank, his heart racing and his palms grew slightly moist as he greeted her.

"Good morning, Cleolin," he stammered, his voice betraying a generous touch of nervousness.

Cleolin met his gaze with her mystifying eyes and bestowed her radiant smile upon him.

"Good morning, Carlos," she replied, her voice gentle as a sensuous embrace.

Their eyes locked momentarily, the world holding its breath. Carlos felt the weight of their unspoken desires, the crackling electricity in the air. He cleared his throat, cheeks tinged with a faint blush, a skittish laugh escaping his lips.

Cleolin's smile broadened, her gaze softening. It was a silent exchange of emotions too intricate for words. Her steps seemed to slow as they crossed paths, bodies subtly inching closer, drawn by an invisible force — he knew it.

Reality tugged them back, and Cleolin continued, vanishing into the elevator with a parting glance that lingered longer than usual — he was sure; he counted the seconds, after all. Carlos watched her go, his heart still racing, a blend of longing and anticipation etched across his face.

As the elevator doors closed, he let out a quiet sigh. The exchange had been brief yet thick with unspoken emotions, leaving him acutely aware of a connection yet to be explored — no, never to be explored.

Suddenly exhausted, Carlos sat behind the doorman's counter, withdrawing a humble *Pandesal* chicken sandwich and a recycled water bottle filled with tap water.

Knock, knock, knock, knock. A tall middle-aged man's fast-paced rap on the glass door awakened Carlos from his lunchtime reverie.

The electronic release went click as the doorman granted him entry.

This is intriguing. The visitor had come to see the Black woman from the 9th floor, the same one who had received the salad earlier. Carlos couldn't help but consider their connection and the nature of the man's visit — old friends catching up, or something more?

As the afternoon wore on, a little girl from apartment 1C returned home from school at 3:16 p.m. Carlos smiled warmly as she skipped through the lobby, her backpack bouncing joyfully with each step.

He wished for her life to be filled with more opportunities than he had ever had.

When the clock struck 6:00 p.m., Carlos prepared to end his shift. But a nagging thought tugged at the corners of his mind — he never saw the grocery delivery man leave. He dismissed it as a simple oversight and pushed it to the back of his thoughts.

Exiting Paradise, Carlos locked the ornate doors behind him; the nighttime doorman had not arrived yet.

Gazing up toward 5F's balcony, he cast his imagined stories of Cleolin and himself into the transcendental realm of his hope.

Then he went on his way, releasing another day for them in the heart of Paradise, Harlem.

Love Is Forgiveness and Self-Acceptance

Oorun inhaled deeply, held her breath for four beats, and exhaled slowly.

Opening her eyes, she slowly reached for the keyboard of her MacBook and typed "Dr. Iyabode Adeola" into the search bar. The screen displayed a summary and a list of results.

When she clicked on what appeared to be the doctor's official webpage, she saw a friendly face that resembled her own. A breath she didn't know she was holding escaped her.

Uninvited, a concern resurfaced: Why do you need to see a psychologist?

She shifted her gaze away from the computer and scanned the room of her local library.

To her left, an elderly man was hunched over a keyboard, the monitor's glow casting a gentle light on his balding head and weathered face.

Turning slowly to the right, she observed a young man—possibly a twenty-something coder—immersed in his metaverse, muttering to himself.

As she continued focusing on her breath, she looked directly across a few tables at a young woman with vibrant pink hair before stopping.

Focus, Oorun! she scolded herself, returning to her research. Because your best friend is right; you need it because you need to break out of this cycle!

Another random thought crossed her mind: *What does the name 'Iyabode' mean?*

She clicked to open a new browser window and found the answer: Mother has returned.

"Hmmm," Oorun briefly contemplated the concept of motherhood. It was something she had never truly known as a foster child and had eluded her as an adult—a loss she deeply mourned. But now, whenever this thought surfaced, she shook it off and returned to the other tab with the doctor's homepage.

Scrolling down the page, Oorun's eyes fixated on something that gave her hope and motivation. It was a section filled with reviews from people who had seen Dr. Adeola. Some described their experiences with reassuring words, while others praised her for her patience and empathy.

Oorun's lips curled into a small smile as she read these appraisals. She felt more comfortable with the idea of therapy and clicked on the "Contact Us" page.

As she exited the library, she asked Siri to call Adrian.

"Oorun, my love. What's up? Are you finished with your meditation?"

She leaned against her car and looked skyward, feeling guilty, knowing that her meditative breathing at the library was not the routine she had implied when she left home that morning.

"Yes," she lied. "Errr, Adrian, I want us to go to marriage counseling."

Silence.

"Why?" He asked, his voice steely and tone clipped.

At that moment she hugged her stomach, feeling the need for defense, for comfort.

Her mind raced as she tried to find the right words.

"I am feeling unsettled in our marriage," she started hesitantly, her words cautious. "I'm not sure how, but I think we need to change," she explained.

His words came in an agitated rush: "If you feel you need to change, why do we need counseling?" He stressed *we* with an angry, mocking tone. "It seems to me that you need to figure out what you want—I know what I want, Oorun. I'm getting tired of…,"

She clicked the red circle on her phone's screen to end the call. They both knew it was the last time they would raise the matter.

***

Later that week, the weather mirrored Oorun's inner turmoil. Gurgling, overcast skies cast a somber, brooding atmosphere as she closed the door to her car and strode toward the psychologist's office.

She glanced at a short, middle-aged woman who passed by her and wondered, *Can she see my discontent?*

She paused outside the door to the doctor's suite and prepared herself for the emotional expedition she was about to make.

"Hello, Dr. Adeola. It's nice to meet you," Oorun said, grasping the woman's hand before settling into the doctor's offered seat.

"The pleasure is mine, Oorun. So, what brings you here today?" asked Dr. Adeola.

Oorun fidgeted in her seat as she sat across from the therapist. Her eyes darted around the room, avoiding direct eye contact with the therapist. She cleared her throat before speaking, her voice trembling slightly.

"I-I'm not sure if I'm ready to talk about what happened," she stammered.

The therapist smiled gently, sensing her apprehension. "Take your time," the therapist said soothingly. "We go at your pace."

Oorun nodded, still feeling nervous but grateful for the therapist's understanding.

"I'm struggling with my marriage and have conflicting feelings for someone who has returned from my past. I don't know what to do," Oorun started.

Dr. Adeola listened attentively as Oorun shared her story. She spoke about her guilt and sadness over her relationship, the stress of possibly dividing her family, and her longing for more in her marriage, including her uncertainties about being with a transgender man.

As she spoke, Oorun felt a sense of relief wash over her. Releasing all these ideas, concerns, and confessions felt like an immediate restoration.

Dr. Adeola was compassionate and understanding, gently encouraging Oorun to keep talking.

"My husband and I struggle to communicate, and I feel like I'm walking on eggshells around him. I fear saying the wrong thing and feel emotionally neglected," Oorun said.

"It sounds like you're in a cycle of fear and sadness. But remember, you have the power to break that cycle and choose a path that brings you happiness, and likely your husband too," Dr. Adeola said.

"Doctor, I'm afraid that my actions may disappoint some of my friends and family, but I want to make it clear that I did not make my decision to engage in an extramarital affair lightly. I am facing significant challenges in my marriage and felt a deep emotional disconnect with Adrian. This was not the right moral choice, but a decision based on my circumstances and feelings. I take full responsibility for my actions and the pain I am causing."

"You sound defensive, Oorun. I am not judging you," Dr. Adeola said softly, encouragingly. "I think it's important that you take time to reflect on the decisions you made in the past and those you have yet to make, and recognize their consequences, no matter how difficult they may be."

Oorun felt conflicted and scared.

"What else?" The doctor probed.

Oorun paused for a long time. The doctor waited, listening.

"I have always wanted children. Adrian never did. At the beginning of our marriage, I felt okay with this. But over the years…" Oorun began.

"I see," Dr. Adeola nodded empathetically, encouraging Oorun to continue.

"Adrian will never change his mind, I know that. Norm wants kids. Because he's transgender, he wants to adopt. This is very attractive to me; this idea of being with someone who cares about professional success, feels he needs to do more in the community, and wants to have a family—I think about this, about him."

Opening her arms, stretching out, palms motioning a pull, Oorun adds, "I feel this force. I dreamt of him before we met. I feel it's my destiny calling."

The doctor nodded, her expression not conveying any critique.

Dr. Adeola observed, "It seems as though your head has turned. A life with this other person seems attractive since he appears to be in sync with you."

In a measured tone, she softly adds, "Oorun, know that, very much like how it started with you and Adrian, people look for all the reasons a relationship is perfect at the start. But living day to day with a person reveals cracks you may or may not want to live with. No one and no relationship is perfect, I'm sure you know."

Oorun paused, her eyes filled with uncertainty. She was sitting in a pool of nervousness and fear. Still, she felt a powerful motivation to explain her reasoning.

"You're right, doctor. I understand that, but I can't help but feel this connection with Norm is different. It's like…it's like he completes a part of me I never knew was missing. I know risks and unknowns exist, but I can't ignore this draw."

Dr. Adeola leaned forward, her expression compassionate. "It's clear you're at a crossroads, Oorun. Exploring your feelings and understanding what truly matters to you is essential."

Oorun leaned forward, her eyes locked onto Dr. Adeola's.

"You see, Dr. Adeola, on the other side, it's like Adrian is holding on so tightly to this concept of a lifelong marriage. It's not about the depth of our connection or a lifelong partnership; it's about the institution of marriage itself. It's almost as if being married is his claim to fame, something he parades to the world.

But I feel like I'm the trophy in the display case. I want more than just a title."

Dr. Adeola nodded, her expression encouraging. "I understand you're looking for a deeper connection and fulfillment. Can you tell me more about what you envision for your relationship with Adrian?"

Oorun took a deep breath before continuing, her voice steady. "I want us to be full partners, not just husband and wife on paper. I want us to explore life together, to grow and evolve as a couple, and to go after shared dreams and aspirations. I feel like he's content with the way things are, but I'm yearning for more, for a deeper connection that transcends the marriage certificate."

Dr. Adeola leaned in, her warm gaze unwavering. "It's clear that you're seeking a profound and meaningful partnership. Your desire for growth and shared aspirations is valid, and it's essential to communicate these feelings with Adrian."

She continued. "Listen, Oorun. Have you and Adrian ever thought about marriage counseling? It's a powerful tool for couples on a commitment journey together. It's not a sign of failure but an opportunity to invite a skilled guide into your sacred space to help you navigate the next chapter of your love story. Since we have started our sessions, the couples therapy must be with another psychologist. What do you think? Is that a possibility?"

Oorun remembered Adrian's response to that suggestion the other day and knew he was not the type of man to be open to this kind of help.

"We have talked about it—once. Adrian believes I need help. He says he is fine, and we are fine."

"Well, Oorun, it's clear that both of you have different perspectives on this. It's essential to respect each other's viewpoints," Dr. Adeola said after nodding thoughtfully.

A sound machine played the sound of a soft wind rustling through leaves.

"Oorun, our time is up today, but I will reflect on our discussion. We can continue our conversation next week, and perhaps we can explore ways to bridge this gap and find a path forward that works for all of you."

When Oorun stepped out of the doctor's office, she saw the weather had changed. A clear, bright blue sky had replaced the storm clouds.

Trust yourself, woman. Be brave, she coached herself.

Looking down now from the hopeful sky, she dialed Norm's number.

Scarlet Ibis James

Love Of My Mother's Mother

Aisha always roamed the rocky shore of her chilly seaside village. She stayed outside for long periods. She never wanted to return too soon to the sadness that shrouded the place that was her home. That day, she discovered a compass washed up on the shore.

Don't pick up what you did not put down. The voice of her grandmother rose in her mind.

But the warning did not stop her.

Looking at it, she observed its needle spun in a staccato tempo, not pointing north. *Well, that's curious,* she thought. *Where are you indicating I should go?*

She pocketed her find and continued home.

All the candles in the house flickered away from Aisha as she entered the room, seeming to betray she had something foreign. Her grandmother's eyes snapped to the child who had been in her care since the girl was an orphaned baby.

Aisha's eyes widened in an unasked question as she observed her grandmother's lips, thin and pursed.

The old woman's aura told of bitterness. Aisha felt the eyes follow her with disdainful slowness. She put away her heavy overcoat and settled into a chair at the kitchen table.

"Gran, what's the matter?" she said with the utmost deference.

The creases on her grandmother's forehead formed a map of disapproving thoughts.

"It's not that I hate you, my child. I hate what you are going to become."

Aisha's hand moved to her skirt pocket. Her fingers clutched the compass, draining the blood from her knuckles.

"What am I to become, Gran?" she asked, her eyebrows knotted as she tried to understand the meaning.

"The same as your mother, it seems."

"Gran, you are scaring me. What do you mean?"

"A letter came in the mail for you today. You did not tell me you applied to a school far away."

Aisha's heart leaped with joy, tinged with some trepidation. She had wanted to escape this dismal village, which her grandmother dominated. Melancholy wrapped itself around this home. She applied to the University of the West Indies — a school on a tropical island that called to her heart. She wanted to be in a sunny, happy place.

"Oh," is all she dared to say.

"Your slut of a mother left me when she was your age too, spread her legs for some random man, died, and sent you for me. I hoped you would be different—better."

Tears stung Aisha's eyes as the daggers in her grandmother's words pierced her heart. She had heard this hurtful declaration before, but it has yet to lose its brutality. She remained still with her eyes lowered.

Raising her voice, her grandmother asked, "Well, you have nothing to say?"

Aisha fished the compass out of her pocket with trembling hands. Then, she opened her palm towards the old woman.

At the same time, they both looked down at it. The wild motion Aisha had seen earlier had ceased, and the device now indicated the true north.

Aisha changed course. Though still soft-spoken, her next words carried a weight of conviction. "Thank you for all you have done for me. Yes, my destiny is pointing me away from you. I hope we do not part on angry terms. Please grant me your blessings, Gran."

Haaawk! Before Aisha could react, her grandmother made a low, squelching sound. Her cheek muscles moved, and a disgusting glob of saliva landed right between the girl's eyes.

In the spittle was the weight of the pain of abandonment her grandmother carried. It was also laced with the preemptive pain from her granddaughter's departure.

Aisha felt all of it. And, this time, she would listen to her grandmother's warning. *Don't pick up what you did not put down.*

Opening her eyes after what seemed like an eternity, Aisha picked up one of the red and yellowed-white cotton napkins from the worn and weathered table. With purposeful movements, she wiped her face off what her grandmother had put down.

She rose, picked up the compass, walked out of the door, and left the only life she had known.

Hot Subway, Love

The air outside was unusually cool for the middle of the summer in New York City.

What a pleasant surprise, I thought, smiling at no one in particular.

This is going to be a great day, right? I asked, trying to convince myself.

I can almost hear my brother saying, Yes, *mi hermano*, dancing in Washington Square Park is just what you need. You love to dance!

The cool breeze gently passed through my thin, white cotton shirt, adorned with playful prints of tiny flamingos and palm trees, enhancing the lightness of my mood.

However, as soon as I descended the subway stairs, the atmosphere changed drastically.

The air turned hot, damp, and unpleasantly odorous. I hurriedly walked deep onto the platform, aiming to position myself at the back of the train upon arrival at my stop. The sweltering heat caused beads of sweat to trickle, making a slow path down my neck. It moistened the fabric of my once crisp shirt, which now clung uncomfortably to my back, chest, and armpits.

Longing for the approaching train to bring some relief, I leaned forward and peered down the track.

Dismayed, I saw there was no train in sight for me.

I took a deep breath, immediately regretting it. The oppressive air flooded my lungs. *This was going to be a bad day.*

As I stood upright, I had nothing to do but wait. I lazily glanced at the opposite platform and observed the crowd—a Hispanic family, Black subway dancers, and young White gentrifiers. However, my attention was unexpectedly drawn to someone specific.

"Julie?!" I whispered in shock.

***

"I'm sorry, Damon. I didn't mean for this to happen," she said.

At least her voice was thick with sadness.

It was of no comfort to me, though. Her words squeezed my heart mercilessly.

"Leave then, GO!" I barked at her, saying words I did not mean at all.

She backed away, taking one trembling step after another, glancing at me momentarily before turning and running — out of my life.

***

Unlike that day years ago, no tears were streaming down her face today.

She looked spectacular.

I could feel my heart constricting again like it did that day.

You're not over her yet? My brother's imaginary voice mocked.

Her train pierced through the cavernous hole of the station, ruthlessly shoving even more hot air into the space.

That blasted train was why tears now burned my eyes, I thought.

Julie, my mind whispered her name with a feeble nudge as she stepped into the cool air of the subway car and out of my life — again.

Ten long minutes later, my train entered the station, making a distinct, rumbling sound. This quintessential metallic melody embodies the essence of city life in this harsh, somber metropolis.

Get on, Damon. You don't want to be late — I'm sure your best dance partner is there.

My brother's voice in my head, nudging me into the moment. His love for me reaches through the ashes of his cremation that lay in the pyx resting on the shelf in my medicine cabinet. As was his way, *mi cofrade* carries his love on harsh words that push me to move on, live, survive, and thrive.

So, I get on my train and move in the opposite direction of Julie.

I look down at the flamingoes and palm trees darkened by the moisture on my sweaty shirt and offer a prayer for the day my brother may rest in peace instead of watching over me, willing me to make it a great day.

Love, Lift Me Up

The elevator doors quivered open, revealing a scene from a bad game of Tetris. Bodies jammed shoulder-to-shoulder rewarded me with withering looks for holding the door.

I mumbled an apology under my breath, the heat rising in my chest like a summer scorcher. My smile, usually bright and easy, felt strained as I pushed myself in.

Then I froze.

Jeffrey was wedged in the corner. He returned the intensity of my wanton stare with a look of devilish interest. He was my new neighbor.

Not just any neighbor, mind you. This guy had a smile that could charm a cobra. He had dreadlocks that tumbled down his back like a midnight waterfall. Today, his eyes were the color of the deepest Caribbean reef. They widened in surprise as they met mine across the cramped space.

Did his eyes grow darker now? Oh *Lord Bhagavāna*!

Heat rushed to my cheeks, though it didn't show on my rich, cocoa-hued skin. My brain protested, but I ripped my gaze from his face as I tried to think of a witty opening line.

My Ph.D.-educated mind is usually a master of witty banter. But at this moment, it had devolved into a broken record: *Look at him. Look at him. LOOK. AT. HIM.*

While my brain was busy with basic instincts, my head turned, and my mischievous eyeballs peeked. To my dismay, they became stuck on how his dreadlocks brushed his broad shoulders.

¡Ay, Dios Mío! My jumbled hippocampus retrieved the high-school Spanish from my memory.

A dimple—a tiny fingerprint of destiny carved in his cheek—appeared with his smile.

Stop staring, Marcia! Stop—no, don't!

An irrational urge to reach out, stretch past the people, and poke his facial indentation bubbled up ridiculously in my heart.

Marcia, get it together! I silently scolded myself.

Floor after floor, the elevator jolted to a halt, its doors springing wide open. The human Tetris formation shuffled out a bit at a time. They muttered about inconsiderate elevator hogs. Also, they pushed me further back towards him as I made way for them to exit.

Then, we're alone in the cavity.

Jeffrey and Marcia, sitting in a tree, k-i-s-s-i-n-g.

"Shoot!" The audible sign of my frustration with my wayward thoughts escaped me.

The ancient elevator inched skyward with a groan, and each floor sounded and felt like a labored sigh.

I closed my eyes, and a shocking reel started.

***

I was beneath him. I reached up, my hands cupping the sides of his head, grabbing his face, I pulled it down to meet my eager lips.

I strained my abdominal muscles to lift my upper body and jotted my chin up.

When we were a whisper apart, he pulled my lower lip into his mouth and bit me gently. I cried out with delight. I felt the shock of the claim echoing through me.

My hands moved up and into his locs and my fingers curled around greedy handfuls of his hair. I pulled him in with urgency and whispered breathlessly, "Come, lover."

He did.

His heavy body pinned me to the mattress. The bed creaked, and his hands cupped my butt, arching me.

"Jeffrey," came out as a groan that escaped my person.

I felt him.

My pupils dilated behind tightly closed eyelids and my whole body shuddered.

***

Ding.

The doors of the elevators opened, and so did my eyes.

The daydream evaporated, but the feelings remained all over me.

Suddenly, I was acutely aware of how close we stood. There was no reason for it, the crowd had departed.

I shifted from one Birkenstock slipper to the other. My heart hammered against my ribs like a hummingbird trapped in a cage.

After I made no move to exit, he said, "This is us."

I looked up to see the lift was indeed on our floor.

But then, instead of my legs moving, my mind caused words to tumble out in a breathless rush.

"Hi," I yelled, my voice betraying a nervous hitch. "I'm Marcia, your…" My voice trailed off, searching for an excuse, any excuse, to get a conversation started.

Neither of us moved.

And the mechanical doors mercifully ground to close us in.

Love, Mystical and Destined

Friday, 7:00 PM

Senzada sat in her cozy living room, sipping on her evening tea. It had been a long day at work, and she looked forward to some downtime.

She continued an activity she had started the past weekend: emptying a small cabinet of documents that belonged to her mother.

Curious to see if there was more to discover, Senzada ran her fingers along the back of the cabinet. Suddenly, her fingertips brushed against a slight ridge in the wood. She pressed gently, and to her surprise, a small, hidden compartment popped open with a soft click.

Senzada found a neatly tied bundle of letters inside the compartment, each still sealed. She carefully pulled them out, her heart racing with excitement and a touch of apprehension. The letters were all addressed to her, and they were from a pen pal she exchanged letters with when she was a tween, Alex.

Senzada's mind raced with questions. Why had her mother kept these letters hidden? What secrets did they hold?

She took a deep breath, untied the bundle, and reached for the ceramic letter opener. She tore open the first dusty note.

As the words unfurled under her gaze, she realized Alex had continued writing to her for years after she thought they lost touch. He poured his heart out in these letters, never knowing she hadn't received them.

One note caused tears to well up in Senzada's eyes. She felt a profound connection ignite for the boy she once knew, only now realizing the depth of his feelings and the impact of their correspondence on him.

Dear Senzada,

This might sound silly, but I believe we are destined to be together. Whenever I get your letters, I feel like the happiest boy in the world. I think about you all the time and can't wait until we meet in person.

My mom says real love can last forever, and I know she's right because I can feel it in my heart. Even though we are far apart, I promise one day, we will be together. I'll come and find you, no matter what.

Forever your friend (and maybe more someday),
Alex

Senzada realized her mother never spoke of love like this. She had always yearned for a great love story, but it never happened. She could only imagine how abandoned he must have felt, thinking a love like that was to be, but then suddenly, he never heard from her.

The discovery of this secret compartment and its hidden letters brought back a flood of emotions and memories, leaving Senzada both moved and intrigued by the mysteries of this past.

She lost all desire to relax. Her mind was curious to know what had become of her pen pal after all these years.

She opened her laptop and searched for Alex's name on Facebook. Surprisingly, she found a profile with the same name and a teen profile picture of the boy she used to write to.

She sent a friend request without hesitation, and he accepted within moments. He sent her a direct message.

When Senzada opened the message and saw the attached photo, her breath caught in her throat.

"Damn!" The word escaped her in a breathless whisper.

Alex had grown into a strikingly handsome man.

His skin was a rich, warm brown, and his dark eyes still held the spark she remembered from his childhood photos. His strong jawline and confident, easy smile made her heart speed up.

Senzada felt a rush of emotions — a fluttering in her stomach churned as she wondered how he felt about her after perhaps believing for years that she had rejected him. At the same time, seeing the boy she once knew transform into this attractive, charismatic-looking man left her amazed and intrigued. She could tell that many stories lay behind those eyes now. She wanted to reconnect and discover more about the man he had become. Still, something in her senses suggested that she should be wary. After all, her mother thought it best to keep this person away from her.

But one idea grew louder than all the others: it was rooted in a heartfelt desire. *What if she and Alex had a great love story, kept apart, then surprisingly reunited like in one of the Hallmark romantic comedies she adored?*

***

Friday, 9:13 PM

She sent the first direct message.

Senzada: "Hey Alex! It's been ages. How are you doing? I can't believe we're reconnecting after all these years. Remember our pen pal days?"

Alex: "Senzada! I know, right? Those were the days! I still have your letters tucked away. We had some wild imaginations back then, didn't we? Little did we know they were so true."

Senzada: "For sure! We went on so many "adventures" just through our words. Those letters shaped a lot of who I am today."

Alex: "Same here. But tell me, did you ever wonder if we really imagined everything? Or maybe...we were tapping into something bigger, something real."

Senzada: "What do you mean?"

Alex: "What if those worlds we created weren't just fantasy? What if they were real? I've been thinking about that a lot lately. Before you sent me this message, I started thinking about you, Senzada. Especially since I started noticing...changes."

Senzada: "Changes? What kind of changes?"

Alex: "It's hard to explain, but...I've been living as something else. I've become a sort of mythical creature, pulled into an alternate realm where everything we talked about exists."

Senzada: "Wait, are you serious? What do you mean by "mythical creature"? Is everything okay?"

Alex: "Oh, it's more than okay. I'm a guardian now of a forest that exists between worlds. The trees speak in riddles, and the stars tell stories. I was always meant to be here. I feel...complete."

What in the world?

Senzada's fingers hovered above the keyboard, the cheerful reply she had planned dissolving as she reread Alex's words. She scanned the sentences, searching for the playful tone her faulty memory recalled of their childish exchanges.

Her romance-seeking heart stuttered as she scrolled back through the current exchange, hoping she had misread something. But the words remained unchanged, their strange certainty stark against the light of her screen. The excitement she had felt at reconnecting with Alex was gone, replaced by a creeping unease.

Senzada's heart raced as she read Alex's last message, her excitement fading as a strange unease settled in. She tapped her fingers nervously on the edge of her laptop, her mind racing to find a logical explanation for his words.

Was he joking? Was this some elaborate story, a continuation of their old imaginative games? But the certainty in his tone and how he described his new life felt too earnest and unsettling to be a mere fantasy.

She chewed on her lip, her eyes darting back to the beginning of their exchange, as if retracing their steps might reveal where things had gone off course. But no matter how often she reread his messages, the sense of wrongness grew stronger. The Alex she knew had always been creative, but this was something different that didn't fit with the boy who used to share his dreams with her.

Senzada leaned back in her chair, eyes fixed on the screen as if waiting for the letters to rearrange themselves into something she could understand. But they didn't. The words stayed the same, and with each reread, the gap between the Alex she had known and the Alex in these messages widened until it felt like she was staring into the void.

A part of her wanted to close the laptop to shut out this unsettling new version of her old friend. But another part, clinging to the memories of their shared stories, compelled her to stay, trying to find some thread of reality in his fantastical claims. Yet, no matter how often she read his words, they refused to make sense in any world she recognized.

It felt like she had entered a room that had suddenly morphed into something unrecognizable, leaving her off-kilter.

She glanced at the clock on the mantel: 9:30 PM. Perfect. It's time to step away from what might be a horror movie.

Senzada: "It's getting late, Alex. It was nice to catch up. I'm going to retire now."

Before he could respond, she closed her laptop and quickly pulled her hands back, as if afraid of being trapped.

***

Saturday, 3:00 AM

Ding!

She stirred.

Ding!

She blinked her eyes open.

Ding!

Who in the world is sending me messages at…

She picked up her phone to see the time.

…at this ungodly hour?

Noticing the three email notifications from Alex that came in quick succession chased sleep from her body. She pushed a harsh breath from her body in a loud exhale and scooted her upper body up and against her headboard.

The subject of the first email was "Proof." The second was "Reason." And the third was "Us."

Her eyebrows knotted as she looked up and down the list of unread messages.

She opened the third one first.

Subject: Us

Senzada,

You've always known, haven't you? Deep down, we were meant to be part of something greater. Our connection was never just about letters or childhood nostalgia—it was a sign, a guidepost to something far more profound.

I know this might sound strange, but you must trust me. We've always been destined to find each other in this life, to step beyond the veil of the ordinary world. You can feel it, too, can't you? The pull, the sense that there's more to our story than what we've been told.

I'm where I belong now, Senzada. But it's not complete without you. You were always meant to join me here, where the impossible is real, and the boundaries between worlds are thin. We've been tied together since the beginning, and now it's time for us to be together, truly.

Please, believe me. You'll understand once you see it for yourself. We'll be free, Senzada, free in a way that the ordinary world could never offer.

I'm waiting for you.

Alex

"What the hell?" She asked into the stillness of her room.

Reason whispered that she should delete the messages, block him, and chalk it up to a late-night whim gone too far. It would be the sensible thing to do, the safe thing. But she hesitated as her finger hovered over the trackpad, ready to sever the connection. It wasn't just curiosity—something deeper, something ancient and inexplicable, tugging at the edges of her consciousness.

Senzada's logical mind wrestled with the absurdity of it all. She had always been grounded, rooted in reality, yet an undercurrent thrummed beneath the surface, vibrating through her in a way that defied reason. It was as if Alex's words had tapped into a frequency she hadn't known existed, resonating with something deep within her.

She could feel a pull that wasn't just emotional but almost physical, a magnetic force that made the rational choice feel distant and irrelevant. The world she had known felt suddenly less solid, as though it could crumble under the weight of this strange new reality he was offering.

The unease was there, but it was entwined with something else—something thrilling, something almost fated. Senzada's breath hitched as she realized the choice wasn't hers. The pull toward Alex's world wasn't something she could dismiss; it was like gravity, undeniable and inert, drawing her in despite herself.

Her heart warred with her mind, but deep down, she knew the outcome had already been decided. The vibration she felt, the inexplicable resonance, was calling her to follow, to explore whatever Alex had found, even if it meant stepping beyond the boundaries of the world she understood.

She knew she should walk away. But the truth was, she couldn't—not really. Not when something deep inside her was humming in response to his words, urging her to see where this path might lead.

With a resolute click, she opened the first message.

Subject: Proof

Senzada,

I know this might be hard to believe, but there is evidence that supports everything I've been telling you. Please take the time to read through these carefully—they'll help you understand the truth that's been hidden from us for so long.

1. Celestial Beings Are Among Us

Throughout history, countless accounts of celestial beings have lived among humans, often unnoticed. These beings are not just myths or legends—they are real, and their presence has been documented in various ways. A recent study delves into the phenomenon: Celestial Beings: Historical and Contemporary Accounts <link>.

2. Twin Guardians Through History

The concept of twin guardians appears in multiple cultures, often described as protectors of the natural and supernatural worlds. These figures have been revered and feared, and their stories share striking similarities despite the geographic and cultural differences. We are twin guardians, Senzada. This journal article is particularly revealing: The Role of Twin Guardians in Mythology and Religion <link>.

3. Parallel Indigenous Gods from India and Brazil

Did you know that some Indigenous cultures in India and Brazil have remarkably similar deities, even though they developed independently? These gods often share attributes related to nature, protection, and the balance between realms. This article explores these fascinating parallels: Indigenous Gods Across Continents: A Comparative Study <link>.

Please, Senzada, read these with an open mind. They're the key to understanding what's happening—what has always been happening. I'll be here when you're ready.

Alex

Her index finger hovered over the first linked research paper. She knew that clicking would cause her to open her mind. Alex had entreated her to do just that.

Why are you open to this craziness, Senzada? she asked herself as she clicked the hyperlink to read the literature on Celestial Beings: Historical and Contemporary Accounts.

She poured over the ancient legends and folklore that mentioned beings from other realms. The publication corroborated ideas Alex had shared with her earlier. The more she read, the more she realized that Alex's claims might be founded in truth.

She looked around the dark bedroom, sighed heavily, and heaved herself out of bed. After a trip to the bathroom, she padded off to the kitchen and poured a glass of water. She looked out the kitchen window, gulped three mouthfuls of the water, and decided she did not need to open the second message. She had her reasons for doing what she was about to do.

With a determined march, she returned to her living room, opened her laptop, returned to Facebook Messenger, and typed.

Senzada: "Let's meet."

Only then did she allow herself to listen to her inner voice: What am I getting myself into? Is this a mistake? But I need to know the truth.

***

Saturday, 10:03 AM

Alex responded right away. He suggested that Senzada come to a secluded location where he claimed he could open a portal to his world. He reiterated that she would have to leave her current world behind and die to herself to join him.

Despite the absurdity of his claims, she found herself torn between an insatiable curiosity and a gnawing dread.

I need to confront Alex and get answers.

She thoughtfully dressed for the meeting, wearing a long, flowing skirt draped elegantly to the ground and a loose-fitting blouse with modest sleeves. Her clothing was made from earth-toned fabrics.

Instincts guided her to showcase her connection to nature and her Bahia culture in her appearance today. Her hair was neatly tied back in a bun.

She was pleased as she took a long, warm glance at herself in the mirror beside her door as she exited her home.

She arrived at the designated place; a dense forest shrouded in an eerie silence. She was acutely aware there were no sounds of crickets, birds, or even leaves rustling. Alex was already there, waiting for her. Today, he looked different from his Facebook profile picture.

Alex was a handsome, dark-skinned Indian man with a regal bearing. He stood tall with broad shoulders and a proud demeanor. But today thick, lustrous hair cascaded down his back like a waterfall of ebony silk. When he saw her, he sat on a stone bench with intricate carvings on its legs and stretched out his right hand to her.

Senzada tentatively approached, and as she drew nearer, she noticed that his face and demeanor fluctuated multiple times. Trembling, she slowed her pace even more.

Senzada sensed something was amiss. For the first time, she considered Alex dangerous; his world may have risks and consequences she hadn't fully understood.

Her heart pounded against her chest.

She stopped now, rooted by fear in place. Her head moved slowly from side to side, and her lips parted. A tentative "No" sprung from her constricted chest and out her mouth before she could stop it.

"I won't go, Alex. I can't."

Alex's demeanor changed again, stretching and twisting with what looked like apprehension and agitation.

"Choose now or lose the opportunity forever," he insisted, his words dripping with urgency. Senzada's thoughts spun in turmoil as she tried to make sense of the situation.

Alex's voice suddenly became louder and sounded like more than one person was speaking. With a resounding tenor, he said, "You've come so far, Senzada! COME NOW!" He stood up now, shouting the last two words.

Senzada's eyes widened.

He's pressuring me. Why is he so insistent?

She felt a knot of panic coil in her stomach. She had always been cautious and measured in her decisions, until now — until him.

She raised her hand, palm facing him, willing him to stay where he was.

She began backing away carefully, looking down at the stones on the path and back up to pin Alex to the spot where he stood.

"Alex, I'm sorry," she said firmly, her voice trembling. "I cannot go with you."

He remained still for a moment before his face morphed angrily. He closed the distance between them in the next instant and loomed over her. Paralyzed with fear, she shrank into herself, dwarfed by his looming presence.

"Please don't hurt me, Alex," she squeaked out. But those words seemed to unlock her body; she crossed her arms at the elbows and then bowed her head into them.

She could hear him breathing loudly, but she kept her gaze down.

"You've made your choice," Alex said sadly.

Then she heard him take precisely two steps away, and an eerie silence descended. She looked up and saw that Alex had vanished.

Senzada collapsed on the floor of the forest, clutching her chest. Her heart raced, and her head throbbed with a painful headache.

She stood back up with a start, brushing off her clothes as if to shake off her fear.

She rushed out of the forest, occasionally looking back to ensure Alex was not trailing her.

As she burst into her house, she acted on another hasty decision she made during what felt like her escape.

She gathered Alex's letters and dropped them into a dark metal cauldron, adding sprigs of sage and rosemary. Then, she lit a match and burned them all.

After some time, her breathing returned to normal, yet she felt melancholy as the smoke from her offering dissipated into the air.

Shoot! Did I act too quickly again?

***

Sunday, 3:07 AM

Senzada jolted awake. Her body was drenched in a cold sweat, and the tendrils of a nightmare clung to her. Her shaking fingers fumbled for the iPhone on her nightstand. The screen illuminated the darkness, revealing 3:07 a.m., the witching hour when shadows held their darkest secrets.

"Urgh!" A deep groan escaped her lips, a primal reaction to the remnants of her dream that lingered in her mind.

It had been a dream of an evil forest, its twisted branches reaching out like gnarled fingers. A roaring bonfire had blazed in the heart of the darkness, casting eerie shadows on the shifting ground. Bits of charred paper danced in the air, carried by a mournful wind.

And amidst the chaos stood a man, his presence hauntingly familiar yet unknown. Senzada shook her head back and forth, desperate to dispel the images and regain control of her racing heart.

In defiance against the lingering terror, she cast off her oppressive weighted blanket, feeling a fleeting sense of relief. Determination surged through her veins as she strode towards the window, yearning for fresh air to banish the residual unease.

But as she drew open the curtains, her eyes locked — with his.

With a jolt of recognition, she understood: Alex — the Alex from her past — had inhabited her nightmare. And here he stood, his countenance transformed into something hauntingly desolate. The sight of him sent an electric surge of terror coursing through her veins, freezing her in place. Panic clawed at the edges of her mind, urging her to flee, to scream until her voice gave out.

Yet, she took no movement and made no sound. Senzada could not tear her gaze away from him. His features were twisted, contorted by a profound sorrow that seemed to seep from his pores. The weight of his grief etched lines upon his face, casting a pallor on the vibrant complexion she witnessed hours before.

Dark curls now tumbled wildly, mirroring the disarray of his shattered spirit. Once filled with life and curiosity, his eyes now held a haunting amber glow, reflecting the depths of his torment. And that thin, evil smile curled upon his lips, revealing a row of teeth defying nature.

Seeing this, Senzada's scream coagulated and welled up within her, choked at first by a mixture of terror and morbid fascination. Then, it tore through the room's silence, reverberating against the walls as her heart threatened to burst from her chest.

The man's smile widened, an abomination of sharp teeth glinting in the moonlight. Slowly, deliberately, he raised a hand, beckoning her towards him. She stopped screaming.

"What do you want?" she managed to whimper, her voice trembling. "I already told you last night I don't want to go with you."

Alex's gaze pierced her being, his voice dripping with an icy gloom that sent shivers racing down her spine.

She blinked, once, twice, thrice in quick succession. Doing so caused Alex to come into a new focus somehow. The weird creature of moments before was gone, and he looked— normal.

His voice crashed over her like a tidal wave—a torrent of contradictions that left her dizzy. It caressed and consumed her simultaneously, its warmth comforting and dangerously alluring.

"Senzada, I— I can't take no for an answer. I am compelled to have you by my side."

His words delivered a jolt, a fiery sting that ignited her senses, leaving her between comfort and the thrill of unexpected heat.

Senzada took a half step back and then blacked out.

***

My eyelids fluttered open. I was awake, but somehow, in a dream state.

"Senzada." I spun toward the harsh yet alluring whisper of my name. All at once, I could feel him on me, around me, and somehow, his words were in me.

"Alex," I gasped. "What's this?" My right hand flew up to my head.

My thoughts played a reel of their own accord. I began reminiscing about the letters he used to send when we were young pen pals. His words would transport me to incredible worlds filled with magical creatures, exotic plants, fantastical delicacies and fascinating wildlife.

All at once, I remembered the exact contents of his letters.

As I recalled his words, I couldn't help but feel a mix of awe and curiosity, just like I did back then. At the time, I saw his stories as pure fiction, made-up tales from a peculiar boy living far away. But now, in the present moment, something shifted.

The memories came alive, almost like giving birth to a new experience. It was a bizarre blend of joy and pain as his letters emerged from my recollection and took on a vibrant and almost tangible presence.

"You remember me now?" His menacing and mesmerizing chuckle echoed in my ear and throughout my body. I could still feel him somewhere behind me.

I shuddered and closed my eyes tight, pulling my lower lip between my teeth and waiting for his words' wave of pain and ecstasy to pass through and exit my body.

"You can burn my letters, Senzada, but my words—I have buried them in you. You are my destiny."

***

His declaration caused her to awaken from the daze.

Senzada's heart pounded as she blinked, trying to make sense of her surroundings. She was in her bed, tightly tucked under the covers, yet she could have sworn she'd been standing by the window just moments before. Her mind spun, struggling to grasp the gap in her memory.

This is the weekend from hell.

She let out a frustrated breath, the weight of everything crashing down on her.

That is the last time I will touch my mother's things. Searching the cabinet and finding the letters was a mistake. I wish I could undo the whole thing.

"You don't mean that," Alex's voice cut through her thoughts, revealing simultaneously that he could read her mind.

Startled, Senzada bolted upright and spun around. There he was, sitting calmly in the shadowed corner of her room. She pulled the blanket up to her chin, sinking back into the bed as she watched him, her pulse quickening. *How long had he been there?*

A flicker of something crossed Alex's face—remorse, maybe, or something else she couldn't quite place.

"There's a power within you, Senzada," he said softly, his voice carrying an urgency that made her stomach twist. "A power you don't yet understand. And some forces seek to exploit it. We're losing time."

His words hung in the air, heavy with meaning she couldn't grasp. She wanted to shake off the surreal feeling that had settled over her, but it clung to her like a second skin.

"You must tell me, 'Yes,'" Alex continued, his tone insistent. "So we can leave this place."

Her confusion flared into irritation.

What was he talking about? I am done feeling weak and led around in circles by this figment of my past.

"Alex, stop this right now," she demanded, her voice wavering between anger and fear. "And tell me exactly what you mean. When I contacted you a few hours ago, we were just childhood pen pals. What changed?!"

"Okay," he said with tenderness and resignation, nodding, "Yes, Senzada, I'll tell you everything."

***

Sunday, 6:01 AM

Get your bearings, girl. Get your bearings. Her mother's voice was always in her head. But this time, Olga sounded very close and alive!

She opened her eyes when she heard this, the words her mother always said to her.

Hello, a *minha moça*, said her mother as she tightly held her hand. I am afraid I do not have much time left. You were sleeping for quite some time.

"Mama, I don't understand how you are here…"

Her mother cut her off and said, *Child, I'm sorry; I'm so sorry.*

"What for, mama?" She could not stand to see her mother in distress.

You must stop interrupting me, child. Let me explain about you and Alex.

"But how — how are you here?"

Senzada! Stop!

Senzada swallowed the lump that sprung in her throat at the rebuke. She was happy and confused to see her mom, who had passed away several years before but was taken aback by the harshness in her voice.

Memories of her mother's gentle and loving nature flooded her mind, making this encounter even more perplexing.

Senzada! Stop! her mother's voice echoed again, commanding attention.

Senzada's heart pounded, torn between the instinct to obey her mother's voice and the disbelief that her mom could be standing before her.

With a mixture of trepidation and curiosity, Senzada mustered the courage to respond, "Mama? Is it really you?"

Her mother's face softened, the sternness fading away, revealing a bittersweet smile.

Yes, a minha moça, she replied, using the Portuguese word for my girl again, her voice changing and now filled with warmth and love. *It's me, but you must listen now. It's important.*

Senzada felt relief wash over her as she realized her mother's intent was not to scold or reprimand her. She sat up and leaned closer, her eyes welling up with tears. "I've missed you so much, Mama. How is this possible?"

Her mother reached out and gently squeezed Senzada's hands in her own. *Let me make my confession, sweet child.*

When you were little, I used to read the letters from your pen pal before I gave them to you. Then a letter came that was…strange, talking about gods from Brazil and India, about some destiny between you two. It frightened me that something beyond my understanding might be pulling you into danger.

I couldn't risk it. So, I burned the letter. I cut off your connection with him. I thought I was protecting you, but I've always wondered if I did the right thing—if I snuffed out something special that could have changed your life.

I'm sorry, Senzada. I hope you can forgive me.

"Oh, Mama."

But her mother had already disappeared.

Senzada lay back quietly, absorbing her mother's confession. The words hung in the air, heavy with the weight of choices made from love and fear. She could feel the protective instinct in every syllable, her mother's desire to keep her safe from the unknown, from forces that might have been beyond their control.

She knew her mother's intentions were pure, rooted in a deep, unwavering love. Olga had only wanted what was best for her, what was safe. But that safety had come at a cost. Senzada wondered how many other magical moments, otherworldly connections, had been quietly extinguished by parents like her mother, who inadvertently shut the door on something extraordinary in their earnest quest to shield their children.

She wondered how often the mundane and the practical smothered the spark of something genuine that defied explanation but was no less true.

Senzada couldn't blame Olga for wanting to protect her. But she also couldn't shake the feeling that something incredible had been lost in the ashes of that first burnt letter she had never received.

"I feel love, gratitude, and regret, Mama," she said, hoping her mother's spirit could still hear her.

Senzada's love for her parent grew impossibly deeper. She was grateful for her mother's love, which had always surrounded her, and regretted the possibilities that had slipped through the cracks because of it.

Was it better to be safe than to embrace the unknown, to dance with the possibility of magic, Mama?

The memory of Alex, the strange intensity of his recent messages, suddenly felt sharper, more significant. Maybe there was something to his claims, something her mother had sensed all those years ago. Perhaps that connection had never truly been severed, just… paused, waiting for the right moment to reignite.

Senzada's thoughts swirled.

She couldn't change the past but could choose how to move forward. Her mother had acted out of love, but Senzada was now an adult capable of making her own decisions, embracing the magical and the real, no matter how unsettling.

She closed her eyes, breathing deeply, as if trying to catch the faintest scent of something lost, something just out of reach. The pull she had felt toward Alex's world wasn't something she could easily say no to—not anymore.

For better or worse, the choice was now hers alone.

*****

Sunday, 6:01 PM

The sound of beads and bells emitting a soft, melodic tinkling and delicate chiming as they clicked gently against one another woke Senzada up hours later. That was how she heard what her mother had left her before she saw it.

Looking down, she saw the Yoruba amulet on the sheets at the base of her belly.

The intricately crafted amulet was adorned with wood, jet beads, multi-colored cloth, and cowries. It was a testament to her heritage and a symbol of protection and guidance. Senzada received this gift in silence.

"I receive it with grace. May you rest in peace, Mama."

She closed her fingers tightly around it, cherishing the tangible connection to her roots and the love of her mother.

She rose, made up her bed, and floated to the bathroom. She washed her cheeks, still stained with remnants of tears, and after she dried her face, she discovered she was not alone. Standing beside her was Alex—her pen pal, her destiny. His eyes, a kaleidoscope of emotions, revealed concern and apprehension intertwined with delight and resolve—mirroring the complex journey that lay ahead for them.

He extended his hand. She turned, met him halfway and reached for it.

"Do you receive me willingly, Senzada. Will you be with me? Do you accept your fate of paired guardianship?"

Without hesitation, she said, "Yes, Alex. Yes." Then she took his hand.

An electric current passed between them as their fingers intertwined, igniting a profound connection that transcended the boundaries of time and distance. Senzada's heart fluttered with excitement and nervousness, but at that moment, she knew she had found solace in Alex's presence.

A sense of hope shimmered through the darkness that had clouded her heart, illuminating a path forward. Once severed by the forces her mother had feared, their bond had found a way to mend itself.

With no more exchange of words, Senzada and Alex stood, united by a renewed sense of purpose and determination. She found herself embraced by Alex's arms, their bodies connecting in a familiar yet extraordinary way. It was as if their souls recognized each other, intertwined in a dance of destiny.

As their beings merged, Senzada's surroundings shifted. Her room, her home, dissolved into a dense forest.

In front of them was a massive stone bench — she recognized it from their first meeting.

Alex gently tugged Senzada towards the bench. Serenity washed over her as they settled beside each other, their bodies gravitating closer.

And then, something remarkable occurred — the stone bench began to rise. Slowly, it lifted them from the forest floor, carrying them upward with seductive grace. Suspended in mid-air, their bodies pressed against each other, they felt an electric current of longing surge between them.

With every elevation, Senzada realizes that Alex was speaking the truth, and now she, too, is a part of this otherworldly realm.

She embraced her newfound knowledge, ready to face whatever lay ahead, confident in their ability to overcome any challenge that dared to cross their path.

"This was and will always be an everlasting love, Senzada."

"Yes, Alex—yes!"

The End

Curious about what comes next?

Some loves don't end when the story closes. They shift. They deepen. They ask new questions.

Scarlet Yearnings Beyond First Glance

Familiar stories continue and new ones emerge, revealing what happens after desire meets time, truth, and consequence.

If Scarlet Yearnings stirred something in you, the next chapter is waiting.

Scarlet Yearnings Beyond First Glance is available everywhere books are sold.

• • •

Get Beyond First Glance

Acknowledgments

I'm deeply grateful to those whose kind words, thoughtful feedback, and affirmations, such as, 'Your work is so dang good and emotionally rich—truly one of my favorites,' did more than contribute; they fueled the completion of this work.

First and foremost, thanks to my husband, D. Joseph, whose patience never wavered, even when my words took over our lives. Your quiet encouragement has been the steady presence walking alongside me through this journey.

To my writing advisor, C. Elyse, for her invaluable guidance, support, and expertise throughout this and other projects.

Crystal Nero's meticulous attention to detail and insightful suggestions significantly enhanced the clarity and impact of this book. I am profoundly grateful for her exceptional editing skills.

Additionally, a heartfelt thank you goes out to the dedicated followers of my stories on Medium.com and Substack. Your consistent readership, especially those who always offered insightful commentary and encouraging words, significantly motivated me to bring these stories together in this format. Your feedback and support were invaluable.

Lastly, I want to acknowledge Bruce Coulter, David Perlmutter, Debdutta Pal, Edward Swafford, Henery X, Jessica Levine, JF Danskin, Mehmet Yildiz, Mitch, Susi Moore and Toni Greathouse. Because of you, this book is a published gift for all.

A Note from The Author

Thank You for Reading!

Your support means the world to me.

If you enjoyed *Scarlet Yearnings: Stories of Love and Desire*, please consider leaving a review on Amazon, Goodreads, or wherever you discovered this book.

Your feedback helps other readers find their next favorite read and inspires me to keep writing stories that resonate with you.

Visit www.scarletibisjames.com for updates, book talks, and more!

Aşę,
Scarlet Ibis James

@scarlet.ibis.james
www.scarletibisjames.com

About the Author

Scarlet Ibis James crafts stories where Caribbean spirits intertwine with Harlem's rhythms, drawing deep from her Trinidadian roots and her life in New York City.

Known for weaving intergenerational tales that pulse with soca rhythms and city beats, James explores how love, culture, and destiny reflect across oceans and decades. Her characters navigate the spaces between islands and boroughs, between traditional expectations and personal truth, creating stories that feel like conversations with your boldest friend – the one who understands that sometimes the bravest thing we can do is choose differently than those who came before us.

When not writing about love's many faces, James can be found hunting down the perfect roti in Queens, swaying to calypso in her Harlem apartment-turned-writing-sanctuary, or collecting stories while people-watching on subways and in parks. She believes every tale holds a touch of ancestral knowing, whether it blooms in Port of Spain's frangipani or poui trees or sprouts through the cracks of New York City sidewalks.

Her writing celebrates the complexity of Caribbean-American identity, the power of inherited stories, and the courage it takes to break cycles and forge new paths. For James, inspiration flows from everywhere – family histories whispered over morning coffee, steelpan rhythms floating on island breezes when she visits home, and the endless possibilities in her American city built where the spirits of the Wecquaesgeek people still rise.

Keep up with her at www.scarletibisjames.com.

More from Scarlet Ibis James

Scarlet Birthright: What They Left Behind

"An emotionally resonant intergenerational story of love, absence, and forgiveness ... grounded, affecting, and quietly powerful." — Foreword Reviews

Set in Trinidad, Scarlet Birthright follows three generations bound by passion, regret, and renewal. A mother's bright spirit, a father's divided heart, and a daughter raised by loving grandparents weave a tapestry of longing and liberation, proving that even deep scars can bloom into enduring hope.

A Father's Choice + A Daughter's Fate

Love in the Dark: A Holiday Romance for Grown-Ups

"A warm, tender, beautifully written holiday romance for readers who believe love deepens with age." — The Bourbon-Sipping Bibliophile

When a blizzard traps Marissa and Gregory in their Connecticut home two weeks before Christmas, a long-married couple must decide if their relationship can survive into the New Year. Love in the Dark explores marriage after the honeymoon fades, love after routine settles in, and what it takes to find your way back to someone who never left your side.

When the lights go out, the truth comes on.

https://scarletibisjames.com/books